FATE BOUND

Fate Bound Trilogy #1

Madeline Freeman

First Print Edition: June 2016

ISBN: 1533642206
ISBN 13: 978-1533642202

For information:
http://www.madelinefreeman.net

Acknowledgments

Thank you to Leah at Invisible Ink Editing for your help and intervention.

Thank you to Steven Novak for the lovely cover.

CHAPTER ONE

I KNEW AS SOON as I woke up this morning that today would be the day I died. Call it a premonition or simply a gut feeling, but the same weight of foreboding sat in the pit of my stomach seven years ago. I knew before my aunt Erica even came to pick me up from school that my dad had finally lost his battle with cancer.

The feeling alone should've been enough to keep me from going out after work, but things at the call center were worse than usual. Typically when people phone in for tech support, no matter how irritated they are, they understand I'm not the source of their problems and that I'm doing my best to help. But today, caller after caller yelled and screamed and belittled me, and going straight home to my crap apartment—with no food in the fridge and neighbors who either can't stop arguing at the top of their lungs or think everyone in the vicinity should be able to hear what's on their TV—was out of the question.

I've been to Shiner's dozens of times. It's a total dive—the kind of place where the glasses aren't always one hundred percent clean but where the bartender has never bothered to check my ID, which would reveal I'm only nineteen. I usually only stay for a beer or two and tip as generously as I can—which is partially why there's no food at my apartment. Every once in a while, a new thirty-something man will join me at my table in the corner and offer to buy me a drink, but I always turn him down, fully aware such offers come with strings. But when a blond guy in his twenties sat beside me tonight, I couldn't make myself ask him to leave. I wanted to—it's pretty much my standard rule—but as soon as he opened his mouth, the protest died in my throat.

I'm tipsy when I leave the bar. It's late—later than I've ever stayed out. I can tell it's closing time because the staff has started wiping down surfaces and resting upturned chairs on tabletops. My companion for the evening has disappeared, and no matter how hard I try, I can't recall his face.

The parking lot is nearly empty, and my car is in the furthest corner under a burned-out lamp. I didn't think much of it when I arrived, but the spot looks a lot more menacing at two o'clock in the morning. I adjust my grip on my keys the way I learned in self-defense class in sixth grade, preparing to use them as a weapon if necessary, but the alcohol in my veins slows my reaction time and the metal clinks as it hits the ground.

I should recognize the rough scraping sound of feet dashing across the gravel-strewn parking lot, but it takes me a second too long and the man is upon me before I can react. My balance, already precarious from the alcohol and the angle I'm bent at to retrieve my keys, fails completely as he impacts me from behind. Jagged stones gouge my palm and elbow as I attempt to break my fall.

"Give me your money," he growls, his hands already yanking at my purse. His face is shadowed under the hood of his dark sweatshirt and his breath reeks like hot garbage.

I should just let it go. The bag is falling apart and there's only seventeen dollars and some change in my wallet. But there's also a picture of my dad and me from the summer before he got sick. It's the only picture I still have of him and I'll be damned if I give it up without a fight. I scrabble at the packed-earth lot, desperate to cobble together a handful of dirt. When he rips at the purse again, I spin and aim my pitiful arsenal of sand grains and pebbles at his face.

"The hell!" he howls, releasing his grip and pressing his meaty palms to his eyes. I use the momentary distraction to scoop up my keys and clamber to my feet. The adrenaline spiking in my system clears my head, but my movements are still uncoordinated as I dash for my car.

I'm twenty yards away. I can make it—I know I can. I grip my car keys, wishing I'd spent the money to upgrade to keyless entry. There will be plenty of time for him to catch up when I'm unlocking the door.

Ten yards away. Five.

His hand catches my hair and wrenches my head backward, pulling until I stumble. A sharp, searing pain shoots through my abdomen again and again—three, four, five times—until I drop to the ground. My vision swims as I look up. There's just enough light from the nearest street lamp to glint off the pocket knife he holds as he bends down to relieve me of my purse. "I just wanted your money," he says as he backs away.

I want to call out, but the back of my throat fills with blood, choking my words.

This is it. My end. I've thought about it countless times before. I spent so many nights wondering whether my dad was aware of the moment he moved from life in his drug-induced coma to death and whatever came next. I like to think he knew, that he was prepared. I always wanted to die that way, with as little unfinished business as possible. But this death is far more like my mother's: She was anxiously awaiting the next phase in her life when she suffered a postpartum hemorrhage in the hours after I was born.

The rushing in my ears is punctuated by the steady crunch of gravel. I try to turn toward the sound, to verify it's not my imagination playing tricks on me, but my body isn't responding. If someone is coming and he calls for help, there's no way I'll hold on long enough for it to arrive. Hell, even if this guy is a *doctor* I doubt he could save me. Blackness encroaches on the edges of my vision and it's getting harder to breathe through the blood.

A face appears above me. The man's dark curls are wild like he's been running, and his gunmetal-blue eyes fix on mine with an intensity that removes me from my body, from my pain, from my struggle to take in my next ragged breath. Fear flashes in his gaze—the same kind my dad always tried to hide when he spoke of his chances for survival. But this man is a stranger. Why does the terror etching his face feel so... personal?

I gasp, but instead of air, I swallow warm, thick blood. Spluttering and choking, I lift my arm, hoping the stranger will understand what I need. I don't want to be alone when I die. I want him to hold my hand, to stay with me until I'm gone.

His fingers lace through mine and squeeze. I stare into his eyes, wanting the last thing I see to be beautiful. The gray-blue of his irises reminds me of the sky before a storm, and I want to lose myself in it.

The pain in my body ratchets up. It's as if someone is pouring liquid metal through my body, melting me from the inside out. A scream catches in my throat, blocked by the blood pooling there.

I want it to be over. How much longer can I endure pain like this? I find the stranger's face again and stare at him, hoping to telegraph what I need to him. He seems like a kind person, but if that were true, he'd close his fingers around my neck and end this suffering. But the panic in his eyes ebbs.

Then the color shifts until his eyes flash gold.

This must be a consequence of dying—seeing crazy things. Soon, I'm sure, my life will flash through my mind—although, in truth, I hope it doesn't unless I can choose to review only certain moments. But I'm not greeted with visions of my past. Instead the man's face mutates, elongating at the nose and mouth as hair begins to sprout out of his skin. Something rough scrapes my palm as he removes his hand and slips out of sight. I want to turn to see where he's gone, but I can't. My body won't respond. Blackness creeps into my periphery, covering more of my vision with each passing moment.

The fiery burning sweeps through my body, filling every atom. The force of it is too much for me to handle, and everything goes dark.

WHEN HE SLID into the chair at my corner table, I let out an audible groan. I usually do my best to be polite when turning away the older men who try to buy me drinks, but I wasn't in the mood. Still, he was talking before I looked up at him.

"I'd love to buy the next round." His voice was smooth, seductive.

I opened my mouth, ready to tell him no, but when I locked my eyes on his electric blues, the syllables rearranged themselves on my tongue. "I'd like that."

He was handsome in the kind of extremely-hot-boy-next-door way that made my body tingle. His strong jaw was accentuated by the barest hint of blond stubble, the same color as the hair on his head. He bought me one drink, and then another. Somewhere around drink four or five he led me to the dance floor, where we swayed out of time with the music. I remember the scrape of his stubble against my neck and the warmth of his lips on my skin. I blushed, embarrassed to be kissed like that by a stranger in a very public space, but before I could stop him, I felt a shock of pain like he was nibbling at my skin and had nipped too hard.

Back at the table, I told him about my premonition, how I thought today would be the day I died. He smiled then, and the bar lights glinted off his teeth. "When life is what's ailing you, sometimes death is the cure," he told me before lifting my wrist to his lips and nipping at my skin again.

My recollections of the night are fuzzy after that. I left alone when the bar closed. I don't know where my blond companion disappeared to. If I'd walked out with him, maybe the mugger wouldn't have attacked me. But if he hadn't, I never would have seen the dark-haired guy whose eyes flashed gold. I never would have experienced the thrill of having someone look at me like I mattered. If only I could have met him before I died.

Is this what death is? Will I simply revisit my regrets for all eternity, wishing things had happened differently? There are so many things in my nineteen years I wish I could have changed. I wish my mom had lived to enjoy the daughter she'd always wanted to have. I wish my father had been strong enough to survive the cancer. I wish I'd never gone to live with my aunt Erica, and that I'd never had the misfortune of meeting her boyfriend Abe.

If I'm going to be stuck in my own mind, I want to remember the good times—few though there were. I scour my memory for happy moments, but something distracts me. Something tugs at my awareness. How can I be aware of anything if I'm dead?

Sounds. But if I'm hearing sounds, I must have functioning ears. A body.

Voices. I can't make out what they're saying, but I hear them. And if I can hear, maybe I'm not dead after all.

CHAPTER TWO

"IT DOESN'T MAKE SENSE."

A girl is speaking. I try to open my eyes to see her, but lifting my eyelids takes too much effort.

"You're overthinking." The second girl's voice is lower, her tone dismissive. "As usual."

Other sensations vie for my attention. I'm lying down, but not on the sharp gravel covering the packed-earth parking lot. I'm on a bed. And the air isn't tinged with the scent of garbage from the bar's dumpster.

"Do you think this has something to do with where he's been disappearing to in the evenings?" the first girl asks. "And did you notice there's no mark? Did he say anything to you about that?"

"I know what you know, Lillie. He asked me to sit here to keep watch, so I'm here. But there's no food in this place, and I'm hungry. I'm going out."

"Oh, okay," Lillie says. "Could you bring me back—"

A door thuds closed before she can finish her sentence.

"Well, then," she mutters. "I guess I'll just stay here and..." Her voice trails and light footfalls pad closer to me.

With effort, I manage to open my eyes, but the sight that greets me is so confusing I almost close them again, convinced I must be dreaming.

I'm in my room. It looks exactly as it has since I signed the lease a year ago, from the lumpy drywall patches on the off-white walls to the two laundry baskets—one for clean clothes, the other for dirty ones. But how is this possible? I was in the bar parking lot. That mugger stabbed me. Even if the injuries weren't as life-threatening as I'd believed, I should be in a hospital, not in my bed.

The door creaks open and it's only then I realize the girls must have been standing in the living room when they were talking. But how is that possible when they sounded so close?

A girl pokes her head into the room, confusion and alarm flickering across her face for an instant before they're replaced by a warm smile that reveals a small gap between her front teeth. She's young—maybe my age or a couple of years older—and she's in jeans and a light blue camisole. Her elbow-length blonde hair is parted down the middle. She steps toward me. “How are you doing? I wasn’t expecting you to be awake so soon. I’m Lillie.”

“Why are you in my apartment?” I ask, pulling my thin quilt up under my chin. “What’s happening?”

She perches on the edge of the mattress, and I struggle to sit and pull my legs away from her. “What’s the last thing you remember?” she asks, her brown eyes laced with trepidation.

The brown-haired man’s golden eyes flash through my mind, but I elect to keep that bit of information to myself. No use sounding crazy. “I was in a parking lot, heading for my car. Someone tried to rob me and when I tried to get away, he stabbed me.” The mugger stuck the knife in me so many times I lost count. I should be in a lot of pain right now, but I feel normal. I shove the blanket down and inspect my body. I touch my stomach through the fabric of my blue nightgown, but I don’t feel any bandages. I’m not even tender. “How long was I unconscious?”

Lillie is studying me closely. “About thirty-six hours.”

I allow her words to sink in, replaying them in my mind to be sure I heard her right. “Thirty-six *hours*? That’s not possible.” I shift as I pull at the gown, tugging the material until I have enough slack to lift it. I'm stunned by what I see: no stitches, no scabs, and no scars. Something on the inside of my right wrist catches my eye—two small white circles about an inch and a half apart—but before I can wonder about them, Lillie is speaking.

"I don't want you to freak out, but there is an explanation for why your injuries healed so quickly."

I stare at her. "You're trying to tell me there's a perfectly reasonable explanation for why I'm all healed up less than two days after some dude tried to stab me to death?"

The corners of Lillie's mouth upturn in a wry smile. "I didn't say anything about it being reasonable." Before I can stop her, she takes hold of my hand with a stronger grip than I would have thought her capable of. She forces my fingertips against my abdomen where any evidence of my injuries should be.

A memory flashes through my mind: the brown-haired guy's eyes as they turned gold and his face started to change. It shifted until it was no longer a man's, but that of a wolf. Fur grew in thick, covering the top of his head with dark gray and the underside with vibrant white. He dipped his magnificent head down low and touched his wet nose against my cheek. A voice echoed through my mind: *Marked and claimed. Mine.*

I blink and the world comes into focus again. I gasp with the adrenaline that accompanied the memory. I lock eyes with Lillie, who squeezes my hand.

"You're a werewolf."

CHAPTER THREE

SHE'S CRAZY. This kind-looking blonde girl is stark-raving mad.

"A werewolf?" I ask, not bothering to hide my disbelief. "Sure, sounds legit."

I fling off the quilt and swing my legs over the edge of the bed. I want to get away from her, but this is my apartment. If I tell her to leave, will she? I might have to call the cops to intervene, but first I need to find my phone. It was in the back pocket of my pants and I scan the room for them.

Except they're not in the room. They're not even in the apartment. If they were, I'd be able to smell the blood on them.

The thought stills me.

I stand, frozen in place, as the idea pings through my brain. *I'd be able to smell blood if it were near.* I sniff the air, feeling silly until I detect a hint of vanilla and honeysuckle radiating off Lillie. I inhale again and catch a fading note of sage. It must be a remnant from the girl who Lillie was talking to.

Lillie isn't crazy. She's telling me the truth. I don't know how I know it, but I can't deny what I sense. There's something inside me that wasn't there before—something primal. There's a power thrumming in my veins that I've never experienced—which is saying something, considering I've had to be strong all my life.

Her words sound impossible, but I know in my heart—in my soul—that they're true. The golden eyes, the shifting form—those memories aren't hallucinations. What I saw was real, and somehow I've become the same thing.

Lillie raises her eyebrows as she studies me. "Wow, you're taking this much better than most people do." She lets out a soft laugh. "Jack still teases me about how long it took me to believe. I was convinced someone had slipped me LSD when they first told me. Then again, it was the sixties, so it wasn't that ridiculous an assumption."

A thrill courses through me. My skin tingles in a way that's completely unfamiliar—but I like it.

"Who's Jack?"

An understanding smile stretches across Lillie's lips. "He's our pack leader—our alpha male. He found you last night after you were hurt."

I mull over this information. I remember clearly the look in his eyes before they turned yellow—an unspeakable sadness paired with unimaginable anger. I'm not sure why my wounded body would elicit such a visceral reaction. I'm also not sure why hearing his name would make the cells of my body hum. Is it because he was there for me when I thought I was dying? Or is it because of how I remember him—human him—before he shifted? I had wished then I'd met him under different circumstances, met him before I was dying. But now that I have a second chance, maybe I'll have the opportunity to know him. "Where is he?"

The corners of her mouth quirk again, but she struggles to force a neutral expression. "He's back at the enclave. It's a camp about twenty miles from here—where the pack lives."

I tamp down a surge of disappointment. What had I expected her to say? That he was in the living room sitting on my lumpy, used couch? No—I'd know if he were in the apartment. I settle back on my bed. "Can I... I mean, would it be possible to... see him? I'd like to thank him—you know, for saving my life."

Lillie bites her lower lip. "Yeah, about that... I'm not sure he did."

I tilt my head, studying her. "Then how am I okay?"

She shrugs, offering upturned palms. "That's the big question. You have to understand—we turn humans only as a last resort. Take me, for example. My friend was taking me for a ride on his motorcycle and it started to rain. I wanted him to pull over, but we were so close to my house..." She shakes her head. "He lost control and we crashed. He did immediately, but I didn't. I was pretty far gone, though. And then Jack happened by. He bit me and turned me into a werewolf."

"Bit you?" I study my arms and legs. "But..."

She nods, understanding. "He didn't bite you. At least not so far as I can tell. To be honest, I don't really understand what's going on. Jack asked me and one of the other wolves to stay here with you until you woke up."

Something about the way she says it makes my stomach drop. "Until I woke up? Well, I'm awake. What happens now?"

Lillie reaches forward and brushes her fingers down my arm. Typically, I'd pull away from such a touch, but something about her puts me at ease. She exudes a kind of peace and tranquility I can't quantify. "Now you have a choice. You can join our pack—be part of our family. Or we could hook you up with another pack. Jack has lots of connections."

I weigh the options she's presented. I haven't been part of a real family since my father died. When I didn't fit in with my aunt's life plan, she pawned me off on the foster care system. No matter how many houses I found myself in, none of them was ever a home. I gave up years ago on finding a place to belong. "What if I want to stay here? Keep living my life?"

Her lips twitch and her eyebrows scrunch together. "I've never heard of anyone who did that. Weres... We need a pack to keep us centered—to remind us of what we're meant to do. I can't expect you to understand yet, but you're not the same person you were two days ago. You may look the same and have all your memories, but everything else about you is different. And we can help you deal with the changes." She offers a smile. "That being said, if you really think you'd like to live as a lone wolf, Jack would honor that."

The words *lone wolf* make me shiver, but I can't identify exactly why. It's as if something within me is terrified at the prospect. It must be something werewolf-related because being alone ceased fazing me a long time ago.

"I think... I'd like to be part of the pack. Your pack." I bite back what I really want to say—*Jack's pack*. I know it's crazy, but I want to see him again. I want to feel his gaze on me when I'm not about to die. Will he look at me the same way as he did the other night? Or was I completely imagining things?

Lillie grins broadly. "Good. I'm so glad." She springs off the bed and pulls a phone from her back pocket. "Let me just call Mel..." She taps the screen and puts the device to her ear. From my spot on the mattress, I can hear the line ringing.

"Hello?" I recognize the voice on the other end. It's the same girl who was in the apartment when I woke up.

"She's awake."

A snort sounds. "You're cracked. It hasn't even been two days."

"I understand, but that doesn't change the fact that I just had a conversation with her." Lillie catches my gaze and rolls her eyes. "She wants to come to the enclave, so get back here with the car."

"I just got my food."

Lillie brings her hand to her forehead and rubs the spots above her eyebrows. "Can you get it to go? Please?"

There's a beat before Mel responds. "Fine." She loads so much irritation into the word that I can't help feeling bad for Lillie for being on the receiving end of it.

She ends the call and tucks the phone back into

her pocket. “Sorry about Mel,” she says. “She’s a little...”

“Bitchy?” I offer.

Lillie doesn’t quite suppress a smirk. “Rough around the edges, I was going to say. But she’d die for me. And I’d do the same for her.”

The words hang in the air between us. The only one in my life who ever cared about me that much was my dad.

I stand and take a few steps toward the small, dingy window that overlooks the alley. “So... should I... pack?”

I don’t have many possessions. Living in foster care meant I had to keep personal belongings to a minimum, and I haven’t kicked the habit yet. I can’t imagine hauling away my crappy sofa or the ten-dollar end table.

Lillie shrugs. “You can if you want. We could throw your clothes and stuff in a garbage bag or something. But you don’t have to. There’s plenty at the enclave.” She glances around the sparse room.

It looks more like a motel room than someone’s home, if I’m honest. There are no decorative touches—no pictures, no trinkets. Just my bedspread and two baskets of clothes. The only thing that meant anything to me was the picture of my father the mugger took off with.

“I guess there’s nothing I really need.”

Something like sadness flickers across her face, but it's gone before it can take root. "Okay. Then let's go out front to meet Mel."

CHAPTER FOUR

AS MEL GUIDES the SUV over a series of dirt roads, tension drains from my body.

I've never been a huge fan of nature. I don't go for walks in parks. I don't wake up early to watch the sunrise. And I think people who go camping for fun have a screw loose.

Or at least I did.

As miles stretch to separate me from the traffic and street lights of the city I lived in for the last year, an odd peace settles within me. I should be nervous. I just agreed to leave my life to join a pack of werewolves, after all.

But by the time Mel makes what has to be the final turn into the enclave, I'm satisfied I've made the right decision.

It looks a little like the summer camp a foster

family sent me to one summer. Several one-lane dirt roads circle around the gently rolling hills. Dozens of log cabins are situated at intervals among the trees.

Lillie turns in the passenger seat. "That's my place." She points to a house with flower boxes affixed to the porch railing. Red, purple, and yellow buds spill over the sides. When Mel clears her throat, she adds, "Not *all* mine. I have roommates. It's really too bad we don't have an extra room—then you could move in with me."

I don't miss the way Lillie's eyes slide in Mel's direction. Despite Lillie's assertion that the two would die for each other, I get the sense they're not particularly close.

Mel pulls to a stop at the base of a grassy hill. A long brick building stands atop it. "I'll see you up there." She hops out of the SUV and takes off at a run.

I move to release the latch on my seatbelt, but when Mel's form streaks up the hillside, I'm frozen. She's so fast I almost can't process what I'm seeing. No human should be able to move that quickly.

But she's not human. She's a werewolf.

Like me.

Lillie slips out of her seat and opens the back door for me. "Let's go. Everyone's waiting up in the meeting house."

It takes a second before I comply. I try to convince myself I'm still shocked by Mel's speed, but I know it's more than that. "How big is the pack?"

"There are sixty-five of us." She closes the door behind me. "Sixty-six now."

I make no move toward the hill. "And everyone lives here—in the enclave?"

She leans against the SUV, apparently in no rush to hurry me along. "Yeah. Most of us have a roommate or two. The alphas and betas usually have a cabin to themselves. I'm trying to figure out who Jack might have you move in with, but I can't think of any cabin with an empty room."

My stomach clenches. There's no place for me. I should be used to it by now, but it still comes as a blow. Why ask me to come here at all if they can't accommodate my presence? I swallow around the lump forming in my throat. "So, what does that mean?"

Lillie shrugs. "Jack will probably set you up in one of the empty cabins," she says like it's the most obvious thing in the world. "Although I'll bet Mel will lobby pretty hard for giving up her room so she can have a cabin all to herself."

I study her expression. "You don't like her very much, do you?"

The color drains from her face and she turns

her wide brown eyes on me. "No—it's not that." She pauses, pressing her lips together. "Well, we're not really close. She can be a little... abrasive. We get along fine, usually. She's just a little irritating to live with. I like things tidy, and Mel has a habit of leaving things everywhere."

"Why don't you just move out?" I may be new to the dynamics at play here, but the solution seems obvious.

Lillie offers upturned palms. "The alphas and betas are in charge of those kind of decisions. I could go to them with a formal complaint, but it's a trivial reason to want to move. Besides, I don't want to hurt Mel's feelings."

While Mel doesn't strike me as the kind of person whose feelings are easily hurt, I understand where Lillie's coming from. I was in a similar situation once in a foster home I lived in for half a year. The girl I shared a room with talked in her sleep, and it woke me up almost every night. I'm sure if I'd mentioned it to my foster parents, they would have shifted things around, but my roommate was the kind of girl who felt abandoned by everyone—and I knew that feeling all too well. I hadn't wanted to abandon her too, so I caught catnaps when I could throughout the day and dealt with the inconvenience of not being able to sleep through the night. Maybe Lillie and I aren't so different.

"Are you ready?" she asks.

I'm not sure that I am, but who am I to keep sixty-four werewolves waiting? "Let's go."

As we start up the hill—walking, thank goodness—Lillie points at the long building at its apex. "That's the meeting house. It's always open, and we use it pretty frequently—almost any time the whole pack gets together. Jack likes to make announcements there, and it's usually our home base for pack-wide parties."

I nod, trying to sift through the questions spinning in my head as we crest the hill. But my mind goes quiet when my eyes land on Jack. He stands at the end of a long, covered porch, and he smiles when his gaze rests on me. His dark hair is somewhat less wild than it was the last time I saw him, like he's done his best to tame its unruly nature. The curls at the nape of his neck are the only evidence of the waves I saw the other night. His gray V-neck tee stretches across his chest and shoulders in a way that leaves nothing about his musculature to the imagination. My fingers stretch with the desire to skate across those muscles.

Heat creeps into my cheeks, and I fight the urge to hide my face behind my hands. I don't think any guy has ever had this strong an impact on me. I do my best to keep my breathing even as I approach him.

He holds out his hand. "I'm Jack."

After a moment's hesitation, I settle my palm against his, inhaling sharply when an electric jolt speeds up my arm at the contact. He smells like campfire. "I'm Ava," I say, immediately feeling silly. Does he already know that? How could he?

He holds my hand for a beat longer than strictly necessary before releasing it. "I'm really glad to see how quickly you recovered. Back in the parking lot, I wasn't sure you'd survive at all. I'm not sure how much you remember, but you were badly injured. I've never seen anyone complete the transition who was as close to death as you were." His gunmetal-blue eyes lock on mine, and I feel as if he's staring directly into my soul. "Your heart stopped. I thought I lost you."

My heart flutters in my chest, and I wish Jack hadn't already released my hand. I try to shake the feeling off. It's just gratitude—it has to be. "Thank you for saving me."

Jack blinks, and the spell is broken. "I didn't."

His words make the hairs on the back of my neck stand up. Of course, Lillie already alluded to her confusion around my transformation, but I figured Jack would have more details. Questions chase themselves around my mind. If he didn't intervene, how am I alive? If he didn't have an active hand in turning me, how am I what I am now?

Before I can land on one query to pose, he nods toward the building behind him. "I'd like to introduce you to the pack. They're all excited to meet you."

I don't know if I'm ready for that—not with my mind spinning with uncertainty. But if Jack is the leader of the pack, do I really have a right to demand anything from him right now? I'm sure there will be time for questions later.

I glance at Lillie, who nods encouragingly. "I guess I'm excited to meet them too."

Jack nods. "That's good. Now listen: I want you to follow your instincts when you're talking with your new family. We need to learn where you're going to fit in with the pack. This will help."

"Okay," I say, injecting a measure of confidence into my voice that I don't feel. Heavy dread settles in the pit of my stomach, the way it always did whenever I met a new foster family. I was forever trying to figure out where I was supposed to fit in. At least I have practice.

"Wait here for a minute. I'm going to go get their attention." Jack pivots and strides to the nearest set of doors, and it's only with great effort that I tear my gaze from his retreating form.

"Don't be nervous," Lillie says, but her voice

holds a note of apprehension. "Just remember, you have two sides now—your human side and your wolf side. We all do. Your human side is reasonable. It can compartmentalize feelings and disagreements. Wolves can't do that. Wolves need to know who's strongest, whose lead they can trust on the hunt or in a fight. Jack and our alpha female are both strong, smart fighters, but they're also compassionate and willing to do anything for the others in the pack. Their brains are tactical. They can see the whole picture. That's part of why they're alphas. We know we can trust them with our lives because they'll do anything to protect ours. Some of our wolves are nurturers and shy away from fights. Some are hotheaded and will run into battle without an exit strategy. We need to figure out what kind of wolf you are."

I chew on my lower lip. I've barely got a handle on what kind of human I am—how am I supposed to figure out what kind of wolf is inside me? But before I can ask, Jack opens the door and pokes his head out.

"Ava, we're ready for you."

After another encouraging nod from Lillie, I walk into the building. Everyone's eyes are on me as I enter, and my defenses go up immediately. Instinctively, I scan the room and take note of where the exits are, just in case I need to get away.

But escape is unnecessary. Some of the girls closest to me step forward and offer their hands. They smile in a way that puts me at ease, and I can't help wondering if their wolves are the nurturers Lillie spoke of.

While I get the sense everyone wants the chance to talk with me, no one presses in too quickly and I'm not overwhelmed. Lillie stays a few steps behind; I wonder if it's on Jack's order or if she simply wants to make sure I'm all right.

They ask a lot of questions, but no one seems upset when my answers aren't incredibly detailed. I'm still not sure how much information I want to give away to these strangers, even if they are supposed to be my new family. I've been in that situation too many times to be confident this stop is permanent.

A girl who introduces herself as Maggie asks if I have any family who might be worried about me. She gives my hand a squeeze when I tell her no, but she doesn't press further.

A tall, pale, strawberry blonde named Fiona and a girl with dark hair and deep brown eyes named Marisol offer to give me a tour of the grounds after I settle in. They tell me they were friends even before they were turned—that Sawyer found them after a bad car crash and saved them.

"It's the best thing that ever happened to me,"

Marisol says with a shy smile.

I lose track of time as the conversations shift from being all about me to being about some of the people I'm meeting. A few pack members recount their own stories of being turned or of their first day with the pack. Others tell me how much I'll love being a wolf, how incredible it will feel the first time I shift and run through the woods.

I'm chatting with a girl named Dakota—a tall woman with long, sleek black hair and an olive complexion—when Jack calls for everyone's attention and tells us to go outside. He locks eyes with me, and while he says nothing, I know he wants me to stay put until he reaches me. I wonder if it's an alpha thing—a few of the wolves I met mentioned how the alphas can give commands that pack members have no choice but to obey.

By the time Jack and I make it outside, everyone is standing in a large circle on the grassy slope behind the meeting house. Four girls, Lillie included, step into the center of the clearing and the familiar weight of dread sinks in my stomach.

I look at Jack. "What's going on?"

He meets my eye and I shiver even before he speaks. "You have to choose one of them to fight."

CHAPTER FIVE

"CHOOSE WISELY," Jack continues. "Be sure whoever you pick is someone you can beat. If you lose, you'll be cast out—a lone wolf."

My jaw drops and I stare at him. Is he serious? I just spent the last hour getting to know these people. I was told they would be my new family. But now if I don't win a fight, I'll be kicked out? This is insane. When Lillie explained my choices back in my apartment, she made it seem like just choosing to be here was enough to solidify my spot. Was she keeping this from me on purpose? Even if I go through with this, is this really the kind of life I want to be part of?

Lillie told me Jack cares for the wolves here. Is this what she meant? I've lived with a lot of families since my dad died, and the only one that came close to being this messed up was when I was still with my aunt Erica and her crazy, drunk boyfriend. I left that situation, and part of me wants to leave this one too.

What if I choose not to fight at all? I imagine the consequence would be the same as losing—I'd be kicked out and have to live as a lone wolf. I've felt alone most of my life, but I can't help fearing what it might mean to be alone as a werewolf. I have no idea what this life will be like. What if I go off on my own and can't control myself? What if I hurt someone? No, I can't do that.

If this is the way the pack is run, I'll go with it—for now. I can always leave later if I need to.

I hope.

I take in a breath and draw my shoulders back before stepping toward the line of girls facing me. I spoke with them all in the meeting house. The one on the left—Maggie, a petite brunette—is clearly submissive. I'm pretty sure I could beat her easily, but I don't want to. It would feel wrong to fight her. There's Lillie, but I don't want to go up against her, either. I like her. She's been nothing but kind to me.

That narrows my choice to two. The tall one with wavy blonde hair is Skye. We spoke only briefly, and I don't know anything about her, but I get the sense she could beat me with one hand tied behind her back. That leaves Mel. Her thick brown hair, which had been loose around her shoulders earlier, is pulled back into a ponytail, accentuating the angles of her face. She reminds me of a girl I knew in foster care who bossed all the smaller kids around. I'd wanted to fight that girl then to make her stop being so mean, but I couldn't.

I hold on to all that bottled-up anger and call it forth as I bring up my hand to point at her. "I choose Mel."

Whispers buzz around the circle as Lillie, Maggie, and Skye rejoin the others. I do my best to ignore the sounds as I move into the center of the clearing.

Mel's russet eyes lock on me and she strikes a fighting pose, with one forearm in front of her and the other drawn back, prepared to attack. I try to imitate her, but I feel more than a little ridiculous. I took one six-week self-defense class in middle school. My dad insisted I master some basic skills before he'd let me walk by myself to school. I do my best to recall everything I learned, but the focus was obviously on defense, not offense. I've never started a fight in my life. I don't want to make the wrong first move and have this be over before it's begun.

The pack is agitated. I do my best to ignore it, but I see motion in my periphery.

"Make a move!" calls a guy.

"Do something already!" yells a girl.

Others join in, but I'm not ready yet. If I make the wrong move, Mel will take me out. I have to wait for the right moment.

"Come on, Mel! Get this over with!"

Out the corner of my eye, I notice as Jack nods. In a flash, Mel lunges at me. She's so fast I don't have time to react, and she strikes me on the jaw. I stumble backward but manage to stay on my feet. When she rushes at me again, I swing my fist, but only achieve a glancing blow. Mel strikes me in the stomach and I double over. She comes at me, but I manage to move backward before she can land a kick.

I put a few feet between the two of us. I need the space to give me time to react before she makes her next move. Mel grins, but it's not a friendly look. She's enjoying this. I wonder if she likes the idea of me being cast out.

She comes at me, but I anticipate her moves this time. She's going for my jaw again, and at the last second, I duck out of the way and grab her wrist. This is one technique I remember from my classes. I twist her hand in a way that makes it impossible for her not to follow my lead. She thrashes, but before she can get away, Jack steps forward and lifts his hands.

"The fight is over."

Mel struggles for a split second longer before

going rigid. Once I'm sure she's not going to come at me again, I release my grip and face Jack.

A smile spreads across his face as he approaches. He holds a hand out to me and I walk to his side, understanding that's what he wants me to do. I scan the faces of the other pack members surrounding us and see expressions of surprise mingled with either delight or concern.

Jack reaches for my hand and laces his fingers with mine. I'm too surprised to react, and he's talking before I can say anything. "Since I told you about Ava's transition, I know you have all wondered where her place in the pack will be. Now that question is answered. Although new to our life and our ways, she's proven her resilience and the ability to think on her feet. By refusing to choose an easy fight, she's proven her first instinct is to care for those who need it." He squeezes my fingers and beams at me before continuing. "I'm pleased to present Ava in her role as a dominant wolf. Her heart and skills will strengthen us. She replaces Mel in pack hierarchy as fourth among the females. We thank Mel for her time in that position, and we will respect her in her new rank as she will respect Ava in hers." He turns to me, smiling. "I'm sorry about the theatrics earlier," he says, his voice low so only I can hear. "I want you to know you were never at risk of being cast out. But experience has taught me that when a fight like this is presented as optional, most people won't take part. That leads to days—sometimes weeks or months—of not knowing where a wolf fits into the pack. But now we know where you belong."

My mind spins. Fourth among the females? That sounds pretty important. Lillie has mentioned the alphas and betas a couple of times. Does this place in the hierarchy put me fourth in line to become an alpha? How can these people trust me in that position when I'm brand-new here?

I want to sit down with Jack—with anyone—and have them explain everything to me, but before I can make my request, Jack is inviting everyone to take part in celebrating my arrival.

The pack disperses in a flurry of activity, leaving me standing in place, unsure of what to do next. Mel is still beside me, and I know I should talk to her about what just happened. I hitch on a smile as I turn to her. "No hard feelings, right?"

Mel's lips twitch like she's trying to smile but can't quite manage it. "No hard feelings," she repeats. "This is the way things are done in the pack."

I release a breath. She seems to be taking this well, and I'm grateful for that. "I'm glad to know we're okay."

She nods. "Oh yeah, we're okay." But her face

tightens and it's obvious she's doing her best to maintain composure. "In the next few days, you'll be learning a lot about what it means to be a wolf. But I want to tell you something right now." She takes a step closer to me and drops her voice so low it's hard for me to hear over the bustle around us. "Your first shift will be on the full moon. And after that, you'd better watch your back, because I'm going to challenge you to a real fight and reclaim my position in the pack."

Before I can respond, Mel spins and takes off at a run toward the woods. As she goes, her body contorts and she shifts from human to wolf.

I sigh heavily. Great. I've only been a werewolf for a few hours and I've already made an enemy.

CHAPTER SIX

IF ANYONE NOTICES Mel's absence during the party that follows, no one draws attention to it.

Jack and a few other pack members head purposefully into the woods a few minutes after she disappears and I figure they've gone to console her, so I'm surprised when they return carrying handfuls of twigs and armloads of fallen branches as thick as my forearm. At about the same time, others begin lifting the picnic tables that dot the hill behind the meeting house and move them to the flat expanse on the other side of the road.

I stand awkwardly off to the side, not sure exactly what I should be doing. Part of me wants to help lift tables, but no one is struggling. Given the speed and ease with which people move along with them, I get the feeling if it weren't for their awkward size, two people wouldn't be needed for the relocation process.

Maggie steps beside me, quietly watching as the last of the tables cross the road. “Thanks for not choosing me to fight.”

I offer a small smile. “It didn’t really seem fair. No offense.”

“None taken,” she says, her voice soft. “We should head over there. Everyone will want to congratulate you.”

Without waiting for my reply, she starts down the hill. I follow in her footsteps, even though I’m not sure she’s right. “What happens now?”

She glances over her shoulder. “A celebration, of course.”

“Because I’m the new fourth female?” I’m not sure how I feel about being celebrated for upsetting someone else in the pack.

“No, silly. Because you’re one of us. We don’t get new members often, so when we do, people tend to get a little excited.”

“Excited” turns out to be an understatement. By the time we make it to the clearing, all the tables are set up in concentric half circles around a large ring of stones the size of my head. Their tasks finished, the pack members swarm me. This isn’t like it was when they introduced themselves not an hour earlier in the meeting house. This time, I’m met with broad smiles and bone-crushing hugs. They keep their congratulations short, but I get the sense that's only because everyone is waiting for a turn.

A warm sensation bubbles up inside me and I smile so much my cheeks start to hurt. A few times when I arrived at a new foster home, the parents would make a display of hugging me and welcoming me to the family, but it always felt like a show put on for my benefit. But not this. This feels real.

Lillie is at the end of the line, and her grin is a match for mine. She holds out her hand and I take it instinctively. "Let's grab a seat."

"For what?" I ask, following as she tugs me toward a table toward the edge of the half circle. As we walk, my eyes drift to the ring of stones. Not everyone congratulated me moments ago. Jack and two other guys are arranging wood into a teepee shape within the stone boundary. A twinge of disappointment courses through me. Shouldn't the pack alpha have welcomed me the way the others did?

Lillie points to a spot several yards beyond the wood pile where Fiona and Marisol stoop, lining what look like sticks up on the ground. Further back are four more people—two guys and two girls—kneeling on the ground, but whatever they're doing seems unrelated to whatever Fiona and Marisol are up to. "It's time for an excuse for some fun."

Before I can ask what she means, music

streams from a speaker someone set up and Fiona and Marisol stand straight, each holding what looks like a short black baseball bat in front of her. A split second later, the ends of their sticks blaze to light, spitting sparks onto the surrounding grass. Marisol nods almost imperceptibly and the two begin spinning the flaming sticks in perfect unison. I watch in awe as the fiery tips trace circles in the air.

Whoops rise up from those seated around me. When the girls throw the blazing batons high into the air and spin before catching them and twirling them again, shouts and whistles sound.

I'm too stunned to make any noise. My stomach tightens with anticipation and dread each time they toss the flaming rods. When they each kick up a second baton, and then a third, I hold my breath, hoping they don't miss as they juggle them through the air.

When their routine ends, I suck in a breath for the first time in what feels like minutes. When I bring my hands together to clap, I find the skin is clammy with sweat.

"That was amazing," I say to no one in particular.

"They've been waiting for a reason to do that routine for about a year now," says Maggie. She must have slid onto the bench across from me during the show, because I don't remember her arrival.

"Wow." I'm not sure what else to say. My eyes slide toward the teepee of sticks and are rewarded with a glimpse of Jack. He crouches beside it, his gaze fixed on something in front of him.

Lillie grabs my knee and squeezes it. "I think they're almost ready."

A glance at her reveals she's staring in the same direction as Jack. The four people who knelt on the ground before Fiona and Marisol's routine are standing about ten yards away from the edge of the woods. The air is tense with anticipation, but I can't figure out why.

A long, shrill moan cuts through the air, followed by a loud *pop*, and an explosion of color erupts over the clearing.

Fireworks.

A lump forms in my throat as more explosions sound. Green, purple, blue, gold. Glittering starbursts fill the sky, dazzling me with their beauty.

They're doing this to celebrate me.

I do my best to swallow, but it's difficult. I try to tell myself not to get too worked up. After all, it's my first day here. It's possible they set off displays like this regularly. But something in the back of my mind fights back. Even if that were true, it wouldn't negate the fact that right now, they're for me.

The show goes on for a long time, and I lose myself in it. I don't remember the last time I saw a show like this. Usually the only fireworks I see are the ones from a quarter mile away—and even then, I only glimpse the ones that peek over the trees.

When the finale hits its crescendo, I find myself on my feet, cheering and clapping with those around me. And when the last bits of color flutter toward the ground, a bubble blooms in my chest—one so large I'm not sure my body can contain it.

I belong here.

No sooner do I take my seat again than new color blazes into view. The bonfire, long since built and dormant, flames to life, towering over Jack who stands beside it, smiling in the content way of a little boy at a job well done. When he turns away, part of me hopes to catch his eye, but he spins to the meeting house and strides toward it without a glance in my direction.

"So, what'd you think?" asks a voice from behind me.

I turn to see the pack's alpha female and beta male, Skye and Sawyer, taking seats on the bench beside Maggie.

"It was amazing," I say. The words aren't enough to convey all I feel, but they're all I can come up with. "Is there more?"

Skye smiles indulgently. "There might be. If we

get enough drinks in Sawyer, he might do some karaoke."

Sawyer snorts. "That happened *one time* a decade ago. Let it go."

"Ooh," says Lillie, banging on the table. "You'd make a fantastic Elsa."

Lillie and Skye go back and forth for a few minutes, naming other songs they'd love to see Sawyer perform. Maggie only manages to get one suggestion in, but even then she blushes and gives him an apologetic smile.

Then the conversation turns to business. Sawyer and Skye begin asking Lillie what I know so far about being a werewolf. They share a look and shake their heads before launching into what sounds like a lecture. There's so much information I feel like I should be taking notes. Skye says after I shift for the first time at the full moon, I'll be able to shift at will. She looks me dead in the eye when she tells me it will hurt, but she promises it will get better the more I do it, and I believe her. Sawyer is the one who drops the bomb about my increased lifespan.

"You're immortal," he says, a grin spreading across his face.

Skye gives him a playful slap on the shoulder. "You have to stop announcing it like that."

"He just likes to see the shocked look on

people's faces when he says it," Lillie insists.

I shake my head all the way through the exchange. "Immortal?" I ask finally. "You mean I can't die?"

Skye sucks her teeth and slaps Sawyer's arm again. "There are still things that can kill you. But our bodies are much less vulnerable than they were when we were human."

"You'll need to avoid silver," Maggie says. "It'll burn your skin if you touch it, and if someone cuts you with it, the wound will take longer to heal."

I nod. I'm not sure I've ever touched anything made of silver in my whole life, and I don't see that changing now. "Got it. Anything else?"

Sawyer shrugs. "Avoid letting people rip off your head or tear out your heart, and you're pretty much good."

I raise an eyebrow, not sure whether he's joking. I don't have a good enough read on him yet to know when he's being serious. "I've been able to avoid it so far, so I guess I'll be all right."

Sawyer tips his head back and laughs so hard some of the people at the neighboring picnic tables glance at him.

Skye rolls her eyes. "Don't mind him; he's crazy." But she smiles when she says it, and I get the sense Sawyer is a guy who likes to laugh.

Before long, Skye and Sawyer leave the table to

join up with some others. Maggie excuses herself as well, leaving Lillie and me alone at the table. I don't say anything for a long while, but she doesn't seem to expect me to. I'm thankful for her quiet companionship.

I scan the clearing. Eyes flicker in my direction every once in a while and Lillie assures me they're under strict instructions not to overwhelm me tonight. If I want to chat, I can venture out and make conversation, but if I want to take it all in, no one will bother me.

Jack has long since returned from the meeting house, and he's stationed at a table on the other side of the fire passing out marshmallows for s'mores. Sawyer approaches and slaps a hand on Jack's shoulder. The two chat for a moment before Jack's eyes flit in my direction. I look away quickly, not wanting him to know I've been staring. My stomach flip-flops and my skin tingles. I'm not sure I like the effect Jack has on me, and I try again to explain it away. It's just because of how I remember him from the other night, because he's my alpha now. But the excuses don't quite ring true enough.

If I didn't know any better, I'd assume the pack members were simply friends at a bonfire. Everyone looks to be around the same age. Sawyer definitely appears to be at the older end of the spectrum—maybe in his mid-thirties—and I'm certainly at the younger end. But I suppose looks can be deceiving.

I turn to Lillie. "How old are you? You said you were turned in the sixties, right?"

She ducks her head, tucking her long blonde hair behind her ears. "I was twenty-four then."

I press my lips together. "So, once you turn, you just stop aging?"

"I've heard it just slows down considerably. But I'm still pretty young so far as immortality is concerned."

"And what about..." I want to know more about Jack, but I don't want to make it obvious. "Sawyer?"

Lillie raises an eyebrow as if she knows exactly what I was thinking. "Sawyer's actually younger than I am, if you believe it."

I'm sure she could go on, but she doesn't. I don't want to ask about Jack specifically because I don't want her to think I'm into him, but then I figure wanting to know more about my alpha is perfectly reasonable. My curiosity finally wins out. "What do you know about Jack? What's his story?"

The smile that flits across her face is all I need to know that she's picked up on my interest in our pack leader, but at least she has the decency not to mention it. "I don't know a lot. He doesn't like to dwell on the past. But what I do know is he's old—over a hundred, easy. He's among the oldest in the pack. His mom was Native American and his dad was from France. That's really all I know about his life before he was turned. He's been alpha of this pack for about seventy years."

I let out a low whistle. Seventy years is a long time. Can Jack really be more than a hundred years old? It seems crazy—but I suppose it's no crazier than anything else that's happened today.

The sky is entirely dark by the time the party starts breaking up. While it's clear there are a handful who will keep going for several more hours, exhaustion hits me hard and fast. I let out a big yawn, and as if he's sensed it, Jack turns from the people he's talking to and strides over to me.

"You ready to call it a night?" he asks.

Heat floods my face at his attentiveness. "Am I that obvious?" I regret the words as soon as they leave my mouth. My tone is far too flirtatious. I really need to watch myself.

Jack does his best to suppress a grin. "I can show you to your place if you like."

I stand, and so does Lillie. I remember what she said earlier about living arrangements. "Who are my roommates going to be?"

"Actually, you'll be staying in one of the empty cabins," he says. "Is that okay?"

I hesitate—but only for a second. Since I'm sure Lillie won't ever say anything about her issues with

Mel as a roommate, I figure the least I can do is give her an innocent reason to move out. "Since everything's so new to me, I think I'd like to have a friend nearby. If it's okay with Lillie, could she move in with me?"

His eyes flick to her. "I don't think anyone would object to it. The two of you can talk it out in the morning."

Lillie's lips quirk into a smile and she darts forward to give me a quick embrace. "Thank you," she whispers. She bids us goodbye after releasing me, and Jack leads the way down the hill.

There's a series of dirt roads throughout the camp, and Jack and I walk in silence down one of them. Now that the sun has set, the moon's silvery light spills over everything. I've never given much thought to its cycles before, but now I can't help wondering when it will next be full. I could ask Jack. I should definitely say something. The silence is making my skin tingle. I keep watching him out of the corner of my eye, studying the way the moonlight highlights the lines of his face. If we don't talk about something—anything—soon, I don't know if I'll be able to stop myself from grabbing his face and kissing him.

A shiver runs down my back. What is happening to me? I've had crushes before, of course, but I've never been the kind of girl whose head spins with thoughts of making out with a near stranger. But Jack isn't like anyone I've ever met. I'm drawn to him in a way I've never experienced before.

I blurt out the first thing that comes to mind: "So, you're pretty old, huh?" I fight the urge to slap my hand to my face as soon as the words are out of my mouth, but Jack just smiles.

"Yeah, I guess."

I try to come up with a plausible reason for bringing it up. "Sawyer mentioned the whole immortality thing, and I'm still trying to wrap my head around it, is all." I take in a breath, hoping I've managed to smooth over any werewolf social faux pas I may have made. If I've offended Jack in any way, his face doesn't show it.

I wish he'd say something. The silence is making my mind go to dark places that involve me learning what his curls feel like as they slide between my fingers. Why am I so attracted to him? There's the obvious answer, of course—he's completely gorgeous. And the look in his eyes as he watched me dying is permanently etched in my mind. But there's a deeper draw that I'm having trouble understanding.

"So, what am I supposed to do with eternal life?" It seems a natural extension from my last brain-vomit, so I decide to ride the wave.

He shrugs and I wonder if I'm not the first newly turned wolf to ask the same question. "Anything," he says after a moment. "I've done the college thing a few times. I've had business ventures. Sold real estate for a while. I've done investment banking on several occasions."

For some reason, his answer surprises me. The response is so... normal. I'm not sure what I was expecting. Maybe something about climbing mountains or visiting the Seven Wonders of the World—not something quite so sensible. So human. "You mean I could go to college if I want?"

He smiles. "Of course."

The idea distracts me from how very good Jack looks when his lips curve. "College is something I gave up on a long time ago. After my dad died, I figured it just wasn't in the cards for me." I bite my lower lip. I usually don't talk with people about my dad because they inevitably ask questions—how did he die, when did he die, how old was I, what happened to me afterward?

But Jack doesn't. "You can do whatever you want. We all pool our resources so everyone in the pack is taken care of. If someone wants to go to school, we always pay for it. Business ventures need to be approved by the alphas and betas. Typically, unless the idea is completely nuts, we say yes to those, too."

I allow the information to sink in. I had pretty much resigned myself to a lifetime of crap jobs and pitiful wages. For the first time in a long while, possibilities begin blooming in my mind. I could do anything with my life. I could even do several things, like Jack has.

When life is what's ailing you, sometimes death is the cure. It's what the man at the bar said to me the night I was stabbed. It's amazing how prophetic the words came to be. I didn't die, not exactly, but I have been reborn into something new. Maybe crossing paths with that mugger was the best thing that could've happened to me.

Jack stops walking and gestures to the one-story cabin before us. "Here we are. This is your new home."

Home. That word hasn't held much meaning for me since I moved from the house I lived in with my dad, but I fill with warmth at the sound of it now. It's made of the same rough-hewn timbers as the other houses on the property, and it has a large covered porch. I can almost imagine what it would look like with some hanging baskets overflowing with flowers and a swing in the corner. "It's beautiful."

There are five other similar cabins nearby, all nestled around a small hill. Jack motions to the one situated atop the rise. "That's my place."

My cheeks burn at the prospect of him living so close. "In case I ever want to come visit?"

He smiles. "In case you ever need me. For anything."

The way he says it sends a chill through me and I shiver despite the warmth of the night. I get the feeling he isn't talking about popping by if I need to borrow a cup of flour. The promise of anything sounds much more intense—and romantic.

He nods once before turning toward his cabin. Before I can stop myself, I've grabbed his hand. I tug him until he's facing me again. There's a question in his eyes I can't answer. I don't know why I've stopped him; I just know I don't want him to leave. I should apologize, but I can't find the words.

The confusion in his eyes shifts into a look so intense it makes my insides melt. His free hand cups my cheek and he steps in close. He holds his face inches above mine for a second before bringing his lips down to mine. The kiss is hard but tender, and I don't want it to end. Something opens up inside me and warmth spreads through my whole body. I want to live in this moment forever.

When he pulls away, it takes a second for me to catch my breath. He looks down at me, a new question in his eyes, one I can't decipher. I want to pull him back, to kiss him again and never let go, but he takes a step away. My skin feels cooler as the distance between us increases.

"Goodnight, Ava," he murmurs before turning and striding toward his house, leaving me to wonder what just happened.

CHAPTER SEVEN

"KEEP YOUR KNEES UP!"

It's been two days since I joined the pack and Lillie has me on day two of agility training. I'm stronger and faster now than I was as a human, but none of that matters if I'm a klutz who can't keep her feet under her.

We've set up in the same clearing the bonfire was in. The picnic tables have since been moved back to their spots on the meeting house hill, and Lillie has set up a kind of obstacle course that I've convinced would trip up an Olympic athlete. I have to jog through tires, weave through cones while kicking a ball, jump over bars of varying heights, and play some kind of demented version of hop scotch through a series of ropes.

I was getting pretty good at each of the activities by the end of the day yesterday, but today is another story entirely. I feel every bit the awkward teenager in gym class as I fall on my butt yet again.

At least I'll learn just how quickly bruises heal when you're a werewolf.

I feel like crap. I didn't sleep well last night. I tossed and turned, trying to ignore the gnawing feeling in the pit of my stomach. I'm hungry, but nothing I can think of sounds appealing. For breakfast, Lillie made bacon and eggs, insisting I'd need the protein, but even though I ate everything she heaped on my plate, it didn't satisfy me. I wonder if my tastes have somehow changed along with the rest of me.

By the afternoon, the hunger has given way to weakness. I do my best to keep my knees up as Lillie ordered as I attempt to make my way through the tire obstacle. But three steps in, my foot catches and I careen face-first into the grass.

"I need a drink," I say, pressing myself to my hands and knees. My voice is rougher than usual.

Lillie nods and leads the way over to the cooler she hauled down from the meeting house. I scan the vicinity as I struggle to my feet. Lillie has assured me no one is going to come watch my training, and I'm glad for it. I don't want anyone to see what an uncoordinated mess I am.

Lillie pulls out a plastic bottle and hands it to me. Before I've twisted off the lid, she's brought her own bottle to her lips and chugs it down as if she's the one who's been doing all the work. I unscrew my cap, but the thought of actually drinking it turns my stomach. It's strange—I'm so thirsty. But I feel like swallowing this cold, clear liquid will make me retch.

Under Lillie's watchful eye, I press my lips to the rim and pretend to take a sip. This has to be my body adjusting to being a werewolf. I bet if I tell her how I'm feeling she'll understand, but I can't bring myself to say what's bothering me.

"You ready to get back to it?" she asks.

I force a smile. "Can't wait."

I really do want to be good at this. Lillie has spent a bit of time explaining just how important my role as fourth female is to the pack. While the alphas and betas are the pack leaders, the third and fourth males and females serve in a support capacity. In the event of a tie among the alphas and betas in deciding a pack matter, I could be called on to cast a deciding vote. If our pack is ever challenged, I may be called on to lead a battalion of wolves into battle. And if something happens to Skye and Dakota—our alpha and beta females—I would be promoted to beta while Cecily, the third female, would become our new alpha. The weight of all that responsibility is more than a little overwhelming.

Lillie and I move back toward the tires. There are only eight of them. I should be able to get through to the end without falling over. Although she's said nothing to make me think she sees me as incapable, I still want to prove to her I'm not. Or, more likely, I'm desperate to prove it to myself.

I don't wait for her to say go before starting my run. I suck in breaths as if I'm inhaling through a wet cloth, but I manage to make it to the end before collapsing to my knees.

Lillie claps. "Good. I knew you could do it."

It's the first compliment she's paid me since we started, and it's enough to bolster my confidence. When I move on to the uneven jumping bars, I feel like I might actually stand a chance against them.

I take in a deep breath and prepare to spring over the first hurdle, but a wave of dizziness washes through me. Pinpricks of black creep in along my periphery and I sway on my feet. A crunching sounds behind me and I do my best to ignore it, to keep my attention on my task. But when I attempt the first jump, my balance is off and I fall sideways, my skull banging against the cool earth.

My head swims. I should get up and keep trying, but I can't make my muscles cooperate. After a beat, Lillie is at my side.

"Maybe we should call it a day," she says as she helps me to my feet.

I want to say no, to insist I'm okay to keep going, but it wouldn't be the truth. "Okay. I think I'll go back to the house and lie down."

"Lillie, can I talk to you?"

I jump at the sound of Jack's voice. He must have been the one who caused the crunching noise. Lillie's eyebrows draw together as she studies me for one last second before turning to our alpha. "Sure, Jack," she says, moving to his side.

I keep my head down as I start for the dirt road. I've done my best to avoid Jack since my first night. Neither of us has mentioned the kiss. I don't know what I expected the next morning, but Jack acted as if nothing had happened between us. I've been taking my cue from him, even though it makes my stomach twist. I was so sure the two of us had some kind of connection, but maybe I was imagining things. Maybe I feel drawn to him simply because he's my alpha. It's entirely possible he kisses all the new she-wolves—and if that's the case, I don't want to encourage his advances. I don't want him to think he has some kind of claim over me simply because he's the pack leader.

I've made it just past the meeting house hill when I hear heavy footfalls behind me. Someone is running to catch up, and I don't need to turn to know it's Jack. His campfire smell reaches me long before his fingers brush down my arm.

I stop, doing my best to ignore the sparks that dance over my skin where he touched me. Even in whatever weird state of flux I'm in, my body is still reacting to him.

"Are you all right?" he asks.

I can't meet his eyes, but staring at his lips is also not an option, so I settle for looking at his nose. "I'm fine."

"You don't look fine. Lillie says your reaction time got slower the longer you worked. What's the matter?" He shifts, ducking down a fraction of an inch so I have no choice but to meet his gaze.

I blink and look away. "Nothing. I'm just feeling a little off today. Maybe I'm coming down with something."

Jack's fingers go to the side of my face and turn my head gently until I'm looking at him again. His brow creases as he scans me. "Weres don't get sick. You're not... avoiding me, are you?"

My stomach drops. "No. Why would I be?"

His eyebrows arch. "You haven't been able to look me in the eye since the other night. When we kissed."

It's my turn to be surprised. At this point, I was convinced he was going to pretend like it never happened. But maybe that was silly—even a little childish. Jack is more than a hundred years old. I can't imagine he'd be embarrassed by what happened between us. And I have been avoiding him, but for what reason? Because I read more into what happened than he anticipated?

He sighs. “It was probably a stupid move on my part. After everything that happened that day, all I did was add one more thing to the chaos.” He steps in closer, leaving barely a whisper of space between us. My skin heats in anticipation of contact with his. “I thought you felt it too—the connection between us. Maybe I was wrong.” He brushes a finger under my chin, lifting my head until I meet his gunmetal-blue eyes. “Your place in the pack means we’ll have to work closely together. We need to trust each other. There can’t be this awkwardness between us, so if you don’t want me to kiss you again, tell me.”

The last thing I want is to never kiss Jack again, but something keeps me from saying that. The burning sensation in the pit of my stomach ratchets up and I’m afraid I might vomit. Great. He’s giving me this opportunity and I’m going to ruin it by blowing chunks on him. “Are you sure weres don’t get sick? I feel terrible.”

Worry flickers across his face and he presses his fingers to my forehead. “Your change was different than any I’ve ever heard of. You turned faster than anyone I’ve seen, for one. Usually it takes at least three days for the body to accept the change. Maybe you’re still adjusting.”

His hand drifts to my cheek and I curse whatever it is inside me that's making me feel so awful. This gorgeous man is standing in front of me, practically asking for me to kiss him again, and I can't. "I think I should go lie down."

"That's probably for the best. We can talk more when you're feeling better." He pauses for a moment before leaning forward and pressing his lips against my forehead. "I'll come check on you later."

The corners of my mouth twitch. "I'd like that." I hope he understands from my words that a visit from him isn't all I'd like, but I'm suddenly so weak all I can think about is getting off my feet.

I turn and start toward my house. I feel Jack's eyes on me for several moments before I hear the scrape of his shoes against the gravel as he turns back toward the gym.

My vision swims. Is Jack right? Am I feeling like this because I woke up too early? I hope that's the case. I hope all I need is a long nap and then I'll be back to feeling normal—my new normal.

It's getting harder to walk. I drag my feet as I continue up the road, and then I stumble. My knees collide with the ground, the sharp gravel digging into my knees. I try to push myself back to my feet, but it's hard.

I should call for help, but my throat is too dry.

I'm so thirsty, but the idea of water or juice—of anything—makes bile rise in my throat.

I need help.

Something deep in the back of my mind tugs at my consciousness. There's help somewhere. I just need to get to it. I'm not sure where it is, but I know I can find it. I need to.

The burning sensation in the pit of my stomach sweeps through the rest of my body. Somehow, the pain gives me enough strength to struggle to my feet. I have to leave this place.

Several cars are parked at random intervals along the road. Lillie told me yesterday that the vehicles can be used by anyone in the pack. I stagger toward the nearest one—an SUV larger than anything I've ever driven before. The door is unlocked and the keys are in the ignition. Without a clear idea where I'm going, I start the engine and put the car in drive. I need to find help, and I need to find it now.

CHAPTER EIGHT

I HAVE NO IDEA where I'm going. I just know I need to get there—and soon.

I can barely see the road ahead of me well enough to drive, despite the fact that it's still midday and the sunlight is bright overhead. Driving like this reminds me of the one time I decided to drive home after far too many beers. I know I shouldn't be behind the wheel, but I also have the sense something very bad will happen if I pull over.

I'm not sure how long I've been driving, but I'm getting close. The trees are thinning. I'm nearer to civilization than I was in the enclave. It's possible I've driven through this town before. I think it's near to where I was living before everything changed.

There's a house on my left. I can't see it behind

a large hill near the road, but I know it's there. I pull into the driveway. It's long—probably a quarter mile. I'm halfway up it before a rambling mansion comes into view.

This is the place. I don't know how I know, but I do. There's something here I need.

The burning in my body reaches down into my bones. I bite back a yelp of pain when I jam the gearshift into park and cut the ignition. It hurts to move, but I don't need to go much farther now.

I climb out of the car and stumble toward the intricately carved heavy double doors. I bring my fist down on one side to knock, but almost no sound reverberates through the wood. There's no way whoever is inside will hear me.

I lean forward, pressing my head against the door. "Please help me," I murmur.

The door beside me cracks open. If I weren't so weak and out of it, I probably would have jumped in surprise. But in my current state, I barely manage to glance over at the person staring at me.

The girl appears to be about my age, with long blonde hair and an irritated expression. "Who are you?"

"I need help. Can you help me?" My voice is weak.

She wrinkles her nose. "I think you have the wrong place." She disappears back into the house and the door hinges creak. I want to protest, but nothing comes out of my mouth.

Before the door can close, a man speaks. "Who's there?"

The hair on the back of my neck stands up. I know that voice, but I can't place it.

"Some girl wants help."

I grab for the handle of the door I'm still pressed against. I need something to help keep me upright.

The man's face appears through the open door. I know him, but from where? There is something so familiar about the lines of his jaw, the electric blue of his eyes.

A smile spreads across his lips. He recognizes me too. "I was wondering if I'd see you again." He steps out onto the porch and slides an arm around my waist. At once a memory flashes through my mind. He's the guy from the bar the other night—the one who bought me drink after drink. He's the one who danced with me, who made the odd comment about death being the cure for life.

Is that why I'm here? Is he the one who can help me?

He guides me into the house and I don't fight him. I wouldn't have the energy to even if I wanted. I'm fading—the same way I was the night I was stabbed. Despite the fact that as a werewolf I'm supposed to be immortal, I can't help feeling like I'm on the brink of death again.

I only catch glimpses of my surroundings as he guides me further into the house. There are paintings on the wall and cut glass decanters filled with amber liquids on small, ornately carved wooden tables along the walls.

He leads me to a black leather couch and I sink into it. "Dinah, bring me a glass from my private collection."

The blonde sucks her teeth. "I'm not your waitress, Luke."

He glares at her. "I don't believe I was asking."

My eyelids flutter. It's getting harder to keep them open. "What's happening to me?"

He traces a strong finger along the side of my jaw. "You'll be better in a moment, I promise."

He didn't answer my question. I have so many thoughts chasing themselves around my mind: Why am I here? Why isn't he surprised to see me? Why is he so sure I'll be better soon?

Footfalls sound as Dinah leaves the room, followed almost immediately by the creak of floorboards as someone new enters.

"Well, what do we have here?" asks a smooth male voice with the barest hint of a Southern drawl. "I didn't realize we were expecting company."

He moves into my line of sight. His blond hair

is almost unnaturally light and spiked in the kind of way that looks effortless. But it's the amber shade of his eyes that captivate my attention even in my current state. He looks at me like I'm some kind of tasty morsel waiting to be devoured.

"Back off, Xander," Luke says, his tone breezy. "She's not here for you."

He sniffs the air before wrinkling his nose, his brow knitting. "Just what is she here for, then? She seems—"

"I'm not sure why you think she concerns you in any way," Luke says, an edge to his voice now. "I don't interrupt you when you're entertaining guests, do I?"

Before Xander can respond, Dinah reenters the room.

"Thank you," Luke murmurs. "Now, if the two of you wouldn't mind, I'd appreciate it if you'd clear out." Something in his voice oozes authority. It's clear Luke's words aren't to be taken as a mere request. After a beat, Dinah and Xander leave the room, both heading up the open staircase behind me. When they're gone, Luke presses a glass to my lips. "Drink this."

My stomach twists. "No," I murmur.

"Trust me."

I want to ask why I should, but before I can form the words, the scent of whatever is in the glass reaches my nostrils. The aroma is warm and heady and it makes me salivate. Whatever it is, I want it. I need it.

Luke tips the liquid toward my mouth and I drink it down in deep gulps. It coats my throat, relieving the dryness that's been building there. I drain the cup, each swallow dousing the flames that have been crackling through my veins.

"You'll need more soon, but that should be enough to get you through the worst of it," Luke says.

His words don't make sense. What did I just drink? Why will I need more?

I rub absently at the inside of my right wrist, my fingertips brushing the small white circles that mar the skin there. A memory flashes through my mind, so vivid it takes my breath away. At the bar, Luke bought me drinks. He invited me onto the dance floor. He told me he noticed me there before, and that I was always alone. I told him I didn't know many people in town, that I moved here after graduating from high school, hoping for a fresh start. After more drinks and more dancing, he leaned down to kiss my neck. Ordinarily, I wouldn't allow a stranger to do such a thing, but the alcohol in my system brought down my inhibitions, and I liked the way his lips felt on my skin. When he pulled back to look at me again, his eyes changed, going from blue to red in an instant.

"Don't scream," he told me. "I won't hurt you." I obeyed—it was like I had no other choice. He bent toward my neck again, but this time, I felt stabs like needles in my skin. Later, after I told him about my premonition, he'd bent his head and bitten my wrist. I remember that initial pain being replaced immediately by a cold sensation, as if he'd injected me with some kind of numbing agent.

"What did you do to me?" I ask now, unease spreading through my stomach.

"Pretty sure I just saved your life," he says, lifting his chin toward the glass I drank from. The residue left behind is red and my breath hitches. Is that what I think it is? Why did it make me feel so much better? "Like I said, you'll burn through that pretty quickly. If you want, we can go into town and get you something more to eat."

I gulp. "Eat?" I get the feeling he doesn't want to take me out for a burger.

A smile curls his lips. "Come on, Ava. You didn't strike me before as someone slow on the uptake. Don't tell me you haven't figured it out yet."

My mind gropes for an explanation, anything beyond the obvious. I'm a werewolf, aren't I? Jack seems convinced. But then what drew me here? Why am I only now starting to feel well again?

"I was at the bar again last night," Luke says, his

finger displacing mine at the white scars on my wrist and tracing a line upward. "I was a little disappointed you weren't there. But given your current state, I suppose I understand why. How'd it happen?"

I should push his hand away, but I can't. He strokes the tender skin on the inside of my forearm. It doesn't spark the way it does when Jack is near, but it still sends shivers of pleasure shooting through me. "How did what happen?"

His lips quirk upward again. "Isn't it obvious? How did you die?"

"I didn't," I say quickly. I want to go on, to tell him I'm a werewolf now, but something stills my tongue.

Luke's fingers move to my face and he traces the line of my jaw and the shape of my lips. "Look, it might be hard for you to accept, and I hate to be the one to break it to you, but you died. Otherwise you couldn't be what you are now."

Icy dread spreads through my body. "And what exactly is that?"

He runs the pad of his thumb over my lower lip. "I think you know."

Before I can tell him I don't, that I have no idea what's going on or what brought me here, he presses his lips to mine. I should push him away. Part of me wants to—desperately. But another part, a stronger one, won't let me. Luke wants to kiss me, and I should let him. In fact, I want this. It's what I've wanted since I met him at the bar the other night. I let him kiss my neck then. What's so different about kissing his lips now? After all, he just saved me. If he hadn't given me the drink, I could be dead now. I owe him everything.

My hand finds the back of his neck and my fingers weave through the strands of hair there. His fingers trace the lines of my body, tickling my waist. I wonder vaguely if Dinah and Xander are still around. What if one of them walks in on us?

No—I don't care if they do. Luke wants to kiss me here, and that's fine with me. In fact, I want it too.

One of his hands tangles in my hair while the other snakes around my back. He pulls my body flush against his as he deepens the kiss. Everything feels so good—so right.

Except it's not. Even as my hands trace the lines of his broad shoulders and skate down the plane of his taut back, I can't shake the sense that something's wrong.

Luke's fingers inch my shirt up, chasing any doubts from my mind. He wants this, so I want this.

Something in the air changes. A scent tickles my nose. I should know what it is, why it's so familiar. It's like burning—like a fire. Campfire.

CHAPTER NINE

THERE'S A CRASH and a sound like splintering wood. Luke pulls away and my eyelids fly open just in time to see Jack, Skye, and three other wolves from the pack burst into the room. And I do mean wolves—aside from Jack and Skye, they're not in human form.

Jack's eyes land on me, and his face twists with pain for a split second before he glares at Luke. "What the hell do you think you're doing?"

If Luke is bothered by Jack's sudden appearance, he doesn't show it. He barely shifts his body away from mine, and his hand is still pressed against the exposed skin of my back. "To what do I owe this unannounced home visit? Were you just in the neighborhood? Because I have to tell you, your timing sucks."

"Let her go," Jack growls.

Luke rolls his eyes, but after a beat he complies. He releases his hold on me before standing and facing the wolves. "If you're this desperate for entertainment, maybe your pack shouldn't have killed Matilda and Leon. At the very least, their misdeeds gave you something to do." He crosses his muscled arms over his chest. "I haven't broken our deal, Jack. And since you took care of the last problem, no one else here has, either. Since when do you not trust me?"

Jack's eyebrows hitch upward. "Is that a serious question?"

I look from Jack to Luke and back again, attempting to figure out exactly what's happening. These two apparently know each other, but how? And why would the pack be responsible for the deaths of two people who lived here? I'm still new to werewolf life, but the crowd at the enclave doesn't strike me as particularly murderous. At least, that's what I thought. Now I'm not so sure.

Several sets of feet pound down the open staircase behind me. It's Xander plus two other guys, Dinah, and another woman, all apparently in their twenties. They glare at Jack and his entourage, their eyes flashing red. My stomach clenches. When Jack's irises change to gold, the shift is comforting—but this switch is disconcerting.

Dinah's lips curl into a snarl. "Is there a problem here, Luke?" Her eyes don't leave Jack as she speaks.

"Honestly, I'm still trying to figure that out," Luke says, his head tilting to the side. "Care to enlighten us?"

The red-eyed crew on the stairs descends a few more steps and the wolves surrounding Jack and Skye growl their displeasure.

"Are you honestly going to stand there and pretend you don't know?" Jack's eyes glitter gold and I can tell it's taking considerable effort for him to keep from shifting into his wolf form. When Luke doesn't respond, Jack lifts an arm to point at me. "What's she doing here?"

Confusion spreads across Luke's face as he glances at me. "She just showed up here. What's your interest in her?"

"That's my business," Jack growls. "Let her go."

Luke holds his hands up innocently. "I swear, she's here of her own volition. Why don't you ask her what she wants?"

Jack takes a few steps closer, still leaving a considerable distance between him and Luke. He holds his hand out. "Ava, come with me."

I push my hands into the leather cushion below me, ready to stand, to take Jack's hand and leave with him. But one glance at Luke makes me question my decision. Do I really want to leave with Jack? What right does he have to barge in here and demand I go with him? Luke is right: I came here on my own. Maybe I want to stay.

Skye takes a step closer. "Ava?" When I don't respond, she turns her eyes on Luke. "What have you done to her?"

Luke snorts. "Not a damn thing, she-wolf. So why don't you untwist your panties and take your furry friends back to your wilderness home?"

Skye and Jack exchange glances and a muscle in Jack's jaw jumps.

"Why is this girl so special to you?" Luke holds his hand to me and without thinking, I take it. "What's it to you if she wants to stay here?"

Jack takes another step forward. "We're leaving with her. If you know what's good for you, you'll hand her over."

Luke lifts his chin, a smile playing at the corners of his lips. "You should know better than anyone I don't respond well to threats."

"And you should know I don't make them idly." Jack's eyes don't leave the other man's face. "She's coming with us. We can do this the easy way or the hard way. Usually, I prefer being straightforward, but as you pointed out, things have been pretty quiet for me since we got rid of those scum-sucking leeches you let into your brood. If I'm honest, I wouldn't mind doing things the hard way—just this once."

Luke steps toward Jack until there's barely a foot between them. "Why are you so interested in this girl? What are you afraid I'm going to do to her?"

Jack's glare is icy. "I think we both know the answer to that."

The confidence in Luke's expression wavers for a split second, but it's long enough for Jack to make a move. He lunges forward and grabs my wrist, pulling me to my feet before I can think or react.

In a flash, the room is in motion. Dinah lunges for the wolf nearest her—a hulking black figure I recognize despite the fact I've never seen him in this form. His name is Duncan; we chatted a little when Lillie was taking me to the gym to practice this morning. The two tumble to the ground in a swirl of teeth and claws. The other wolves run at the men and women on the stairs. Jack attempts to pull me toward the door, but Luke grabs my arm, managing to yank me out of Jack's grip before shoving me to the wall behind him. While Jack and Luke begin throwing punches at each other, Skye runs toward me, calling my name.

I should go with her. I should take her hand and run away from here, away from Luke and whatever craziness is happening in this house. Why can't I do it? Why is this simple act so hard for me to go through with?

Jack and Luke are locked in battle. I keep expecting Jack to shift into a wolf, but he stays human. The thing that surprises me most is the speed with which Luke moves. He's a match in every way for Jack. But how is that possible? How can a human move so quickly?

I know the answer; I just don't want to accept it. I can't accept it. If I'm honest with myself, I've known what Luke is ever since he gave me the glass to drink from.

Why is it so hard? I took the news of the existence of werewolves in stride. Why am I having so much trouble accepting what this new evidence is pointing to?

Because I don't want it.

The realization washes over me. I don't want any part of whatever it is Luke and his friends are or what they do here. Whatever impulse drew me here is not one I want to indulge.

The invisible force that kept me from moving dissipates and I reach for Skye's hand. "I've got her!" she yells, pulling me toward the front door.

As I follow, I watch the melee going on around us. Duncan is biting Dinah's neck. She screams and pounds at the wolf's back. Luke is momentarily distracted as I rush through the house, and Jack takes advantage of that fact by positioning himself behind Luke and snapping his neck in the blink of an eye.

A scream escapes my lips as Jack yells, "Let's get out of here!"

Skye leads me to the passenger seat of the SUV I drove here. As soon as she has me safely buckled inside, she closes the door and shifts into wolf form before running toward the nearest trees. The other wolves head off in that direction as well. Jack runs to the driver's side door and settles behind the wheel. I can't look at him. I can't accept what I just saw him do. Is this what he means when he says he'll protect me? Is this really something I can live with?

I know very little about Luke, about the kind of person he was, but no matter what, it can't excuse what I just witnessed. He didn't deserve to be murdered.

Jack doesn't speak until we're several miles down the road. "Are you okay?" His tone is gentle, but with a hard undercurrent, like he's daring me to question him.

No matter the consequences, I can't forget what I saw. I can't put it behind me and move on. "You just killed him."

"No, I didn't," he says firmly.

I turn to him and stare incredulously. What

kind of fool does he take me for? "I've seen enough action movies to know what it looks like when someone snaps someone else's neck."

He swerves the car and breaks hard on the side of the road, throwing me forward against my seatbelt. His gunmetal-blue eyes bore into me. "I don't think you understand what was going on. I'm not sure I do entirely either. But let me assure you, Luke's not dead. Yes, I snapped his neck." His mouth twitches. "I'm not going to lie—it's not even the first time. But he'll live."

"How could he live through something like that?" But even as I ask the question, part of me knows the answer.

Jack runs a hand through his dark hair, tousling the waves, making him look more like he did the night I was attacked. "Why did you go there? You told me you were going to lie down, but then I sensed you leaving our territory. Why did you go to Luke?"

I try to recall my thought process, but it eludes me like a dream. "I don't know. I just knew I needed help. I found that house completely on instinct."

He presses his lips together and his eyebrows scrunch. "What happened when you were there?"

I flush, remembering the way Luke was kissing me when Jack walked in. Why was I letting him do that? I didn't want to kiss him. The idea that Jack had to see that twists my stomach. "He didn't hurt me," I say quickly, afraid of making Jack feel he needs to retaliate more than he already has. "I'm okay. I don't know what came over me..."

He shakes his head as if trying to dispel something unpleasant. "We'll figure it out later. For now, I just want to get you home."

I nod. "I'd like that."

We don't speak again for the rest of the drive back to the enclave. By the time we pull up in front of my house, I'm feeling weak again—shaky, the way I was when I left the gym. I try several times to undo the clasp on the seatbelt before Jack comes around to take care of it for me.

"I don't know what's wrong with me," I murmur as Jack helps me from the car.

"I'm not sure either," he says, trying to help me to my feet. When it's clear my legs are too unsteady to support me, he scoops me up in his arms and carries me effortlessly toward the door. "But whatever it is, we'll figure it out. I won't let anything happen to you."

His words fill me with warmth. I believe him.

He carries me all the way to my room in the back of the house. There are two bedrooms, and I felt bad taking the larger one with a better view, but Lillie wouldn't hear of me taking the smaller one. She even filled a vase with flowers for my dresser and lent me a few items to make the room feel more lived-in—including a hairbrush, a small mirror, and an unmatched sock because, she insisted, every room needed at least one random sock to prove someone really lived in it.

"Hopefully after some rest you'll feel better. While you're asleep, I'm going to contact a friend of mine. She might know how to help." He lays me in the middle of the king-size mattress and sits down beside me. He takes my hand in his and squeezes it. I try to return pressure, but my muscles don't want to obey.

I find Jack's eyes. "I'm afraid," I whisper. I feel like I'm fading—the way I did when I was bleeding out in the bar parking lot. Jack said he'd never seen anyone as far gone as I was complete the transition. Maybe it wasn't as successful as he'd hoped. Maybe the change hasn't fully transformed me and nature is going to take its course.

He cups my cheek with his free hand and leans toward me. "You're going to be fine," he says, holding my gaze. "Whatever's wrong with you, we'll fix it."

I want to believe him. I close my eyes, inhaling his comforting campfire smell. For the first time, I detect something else as well. There's another aroma, an undercurrent that draws my attention with each passing moment. It pulses with the steady beat of a drum. It reminds me of something. Of the liquid in the cup at Luke's house. And just like at the mansion, I want it. I need it.

A sensation like fire shoots through my mouth, from my gums into my teeth. Jack is still close, but I need him closer. My muscles thrum, and with a strength I lacked only seconds ago, I grab his shoulders and pull him toward me until my lips touch his neck. But I don't want to kiss him. I draw back my lips and sink my teeth into his flesh.

He snarls and fights against me, but he can't stop me. His warm blood trickles into my mouth and I gulp it down greedily. I don't want to hurt him, but somehow I know I need this; I know he needs to give it to me.

Jack struggles and growls, but somehow I know he doesn't want to harm me. I swallow a few more mouthfuls before releasing him. His eyes are gold when they fix on mine, but the color quickly fades. His jaw goes slack and he grabs for the handheld mirror Lillie placed on my bedside table. He holds it in front of my face. I'm about to ask why, but when I catch a glimpse of my eyes, I don't need to. They're glowing, but not the golden color of the wolves—they're blood-red, like those of the people at Luke's house.

As my irises go back to their normal jade green, I shove the mirror away. "What's going on? Why do my eyes look like that?"

Jack's fingers tremble as he returns the glass to my bedside table. "I won't lie—it crossed my mind as soon as I realized you were in the mansion. And then when I saw you with Luke..." He releases a shaky sigh. "How do you feel now?"

I take stock of myself. "Strong," I say almost automatically. I feel better now than I did even after I drank from the cup Luke offered me. I feel far better than I ever did in my human life. "I think I'm better. But... that doesn't make any sense."

"It might, but to be honest, I didn't really think it was possible." He stares across the room, but I get the feeling he's not focusing on anything. "I've heard stories over the years, but I never thought they were real."

Panic rises in my chest. I don't want to hear his theory, but I have to know. "You didn't think what was real? Jack, what's going on with me?"

He shakes his head and turns his attention back to me. He takes my hands in his before continuing. "Did you know Luke before this afternoon?"

His question takes me off guard. "Not really. I met him a couple nights ago—the night I got stabbed."

A muscle in his jaw jumps. "Did he... Did he bite you?"

I disentangle the fingers of my right hand from

his and show him the two white dots on the inside of my wrist.

He sucks in a sharp breath, though he doesn't seem surprised. "And then you were stabbed, and when I got to you, I saw... Still, I don't know why it would've happened..."

It's obvious he's trying to work something out in his mind, but I have no patience for it. "What is going on? What aren't you telling me?"

He brushes the pad of his thumb over the inside of my wrist. "I think you're a hybrid."

I raise my eyebrows. "A hybrid? Of what?"

He touches each of the small white circles before answering. "You're a wolf—I know you are. I can sense it in you. But you were so sick, and you were drawn to Luke. And just now, you bit me, Ava, and you drank my blood."

I shake my head, and the truth that's been waiting for me to let it in floods my mind. "No. That's not possible."

"I don't even think you're convincing yourself."

Blood rushes in my ears. Werewolf? That I can accept. But not this. This is just too crazy. "Are you telling me vampires are real?"

He nods. "That's why Luke's going to recover. Vampires exist, and they're immortal in much the same way we are."

I snort. "You mean the way *you* are. Because

I'm not a werewolf—I'm some kind of mutant."

Jack cradles my face between his hands. "You're not a mutant. Do you remember what I said to you the night you were stabbed?"

I swallow around a lump in my throat. "You didn't say anything."

He strokes my cheeks with his thumbs. "That's not true. You would've heard me in your head. Do you remember?"

I recall the night—my pain, my fear. The longing to have met Jack under different circumstances. The way he began shifting in front of me. I shiver at the memory. "Marked and claimed," I murmur.

"*Mine,*" he adds fiercely. "Nothing changes that. Nothing will ever change that. Tell me you believe me."

I don't want to accept what he's saying. How could he want anything to do with me? I just bit him—I drank his blood. I'm some kind of crazy monster. But he's still holding my face, gently but firmly, and he won't let me look away.

He leans forward and presses his lips to mine. The same heat, the same electricity that coursed through me my first night as a werewolf shoots through my body again. It's as if every cell of my body comes alive when he kisses me. With his lips against mine, I can forget the craziness of the situation—the impossibility of what I am. I'm where I belong.

When he pulls away, I blink rapidly to dispel the prickling sensation in my eyes. "I believe you."

He tucks my hair behind my ears. "Nothing changes. You're still a member of my pack, and I'll still never let anything happen to you."

Cold fear coils in my stomach. "What about the pack? What are we going to tell them?"

"Let me worry about that. For now, let's keep it between us. I'll tell Skye because as alphas, it's hard to keep secrets from her. And I may decide to loop Sawyer and Dakota in. But don't tell anyone else—not yet. Not even Lillie. Can you do that?"

I nod, biting my lower lip. "Just how rare are people like me? How many hybrids are out there?"

Jack inhales deeply before responding. "I think you could be the only one."

Something in his tone unsettles me. "Is that a bad thing?"

He reaches forward and tucks a loose strand of hair behind my ears. "It might be."

CHAPTER TEN

THE PICTURE WINDOW in my bedroom looks out over a small gully carved by a stream that flows gently through it. Birds grace tree branches, and squirrels and bunnies skitter and hop through the lush vegetation below. Everything about the scene should calm me, but instead I find myself pacing back and forth, running my hands through my chestnut hair and twisting my fingers until they nearly get stuck in its tresses.

"Calm down," Jack says, not for the first time. "You've got nothing to worry about."

I can't quite bite back a nervous laugh as I turn to him. "What if I can't shift?" It's the fear that's loomed in the back of my mind in the two days since Jack realized I'm a hybrid. No matter what he says to convince me everything will be fine, I can't fight the fear wringing my insides. By his own admission, he's never met someone like me. He can't know for sure that I'll be able to transform into a wolf tonight—the first full moon since I turned. Since I became a half-werewolf-half-vampire. "What if I'm just standing there and nothing I can do will make me turn into a wolf? What happens when the rest of the pack realizes what I am?"

Jack is at my side in two long strides. He stays my progress across the carpet and catches my hands in his. "No matter what, I'll protect you. You have my word."

My stomach swoops at his closeness. I've done my best to keep my distance from him since I drank his blood. Part of me is afraid I'll try to do it again, afraid that this time I won't be able to stop myself. But no desire overpowers me at his nearness now—at least not one having to do with his blood. Instead, my skin tingles in the way I've grown to associate with his presence.

We haven't kissed since the day he saved me from Luke's house. In part it's been due to my reluctance to be in proximity to him, but that's not the whole reason. My stomach sinks whenever I think of what Jack walked in on. And as much as I want to kiss him now, I need to clear the air first. "I want to talk about the other day."

He takes a half step back and shakes his head.

"There's nothing to discuss."

"But there is," I protest. Heat rises in my cheeks, but I press on anyway. "I was delirious. Had no idea what was going on. Then he started kissing me and I couldn't stop him. It was like I was under a spell or something." I want to take it a step further, to insist I didn't want it to happen, but it would be a lie. In the moment, I did want Luke to keep kissing me.

Jack's lips quirk into a smile. "Vampires can't cast spells. Immortals can't use magic. Just witches."

My eyebrows hike upward. "Wait—witches are real?"

He tips back his head and barks out a laugh. "Werewolves and vampires you accept, but witches are too big of a stretch?"

I can't help smiling. I suppose accepting the existence of witches is no crazier than believing in werewolves or vampires—or my strange mix of the two. "Okay, so it wasn't a spell. But I want you to know I didn't go there to be with him. He's not the one I want."

Jack moves a step closer—so near now that I can feel the heat from his skin and my body begins to hum. When he fixes me with his gaze, his eyes are smoldering. "Does that mean there's someone else you want instead?"

He's driving me crazy, looking at me like that. I slide my hand around the back of his neck and pull his lips down to mine. I don't know what I was thinking when I was with Luke, but I belong with Jack. I'm sure of it.

I'll shift tonight. I want to believe it—I have to. I have no doubt Jack will protect me even if I don't, that he'll still want to be with me. My desire to shift has nothing to do with that. I want to do it to prove to myself this is where I belong. I need proof that I've finally found the family I've longed for since my father died.

Jack pulls away, groaning. "As much as I'd love to stay here, we really should go meet the rest of the pack. They'll all be gathered to take your first run with you."

"Rain check then."

He leans down to press one more kiss against my lips, growling as he pulls away. "Bet on it."

We link hands as we leave my room, as if it's the most natural thing in the world. The rest of the pack is waiting near the tree line behind the gym. Jack releases my hand as we clear the building, but Lillie catches my eye and waggles her eyebrows in a way that lets me know she saw us. She's asked what's going on between Jack and me before, and I've been evasive, but I get the feeling she won't accept my non-answers much longer. Still, when the time comes, I'm not entirely sure what I'll say.

"So, how does this work?" I ask as we near the rest of the pack. "How do I—you know?" It occurs to me now that I've been so worried about not being able to shift because I'm a hybrid that I haven't given any thought as to how the transformation actually occurs. "Is there a magic word?"

He stifles a laugh. "I already told you, immortals can't use magic."

"So no magic word?"

He shakes his head. "No magic word. The moon has an effect on us. It affects all living things, even humans. But a were's first shift happens on the full moon after they're turned because its effect can help you find the wolf inside. You just need to tap into the power within you, and your wolf will come out."

I bite my lower lip. "Nothing more detailed?"

The corner of his mouth quirks. "You'll figure it out."

He motions for me to stay where I am as he walks to the center of the circle the pack has formed. As he begins talking about welcoming me as a full member of the pack, Lillie moves to my side. "You nervous?"

"A little," I admit, being sure to keep my voice low. "Jack wasn't very specific on how I'm actually supposed to, you know, shift."

She smiles. "I remember being so nervous my first time. I was turned about a week into the moon's cycle, so I had to wait three weeks before I shifted. I was sure I was going to throw up." She pauses, her eyebrows drawing together. "Actually, you might throw up. It's not uncommon. It didn't happen to me, but I've seen it happen since. And it'll hurt—but don't worry, the pain fades the more times you do it."

I bite back a laugh. "That sounds a lot like what one of my foster sisters told me about sex."

A titter escapes Lillie's lips before she can clamp a hand over her mouth. Sawyer raises an eyebrow and Maggie holds a finger in front of her lips to shush us.

"Ava," Jack calls, and I fight the urge to laugh again. I feel like a high school student about to be reprimanded by the teacher. He holds his hand out toward me and I take the cue and walk to his side. I do my best to keep my expression neutral, but I'm still smiling. The fact that Lillie keeps snorting with suppressed laughter isn't helping. Jack raises an eyebrow questioningly, but I simply shake my head. He turns to address the pack again. "Tonight, we welcome our newest member, Ava."

A cheer rises from the assembled, and a blush creeps into my cheeks. A terrible thought crosses my mind: Are they all going to stand there and watch me attempt to shift? I used to forget prepared speeches when standing in front of a classroom—there's no way I'll be able to transform with sixty-five pairs of eyes on me.

But no sooner has the fear crossed my mind than movement sweeps through the pack. Some run toward the woods, shifting as they go. Others drop to their knees and change before taking off. Only Jack remains immobile. "Would you like me to wait for you?"

His offer is tempting. If the first shift is really as bad as Lillie claims, I may want the moral support. Then again, maybe it's in my best interest to do it on my own; his gaze might make me nervous.

He smiles as if reading my mind. "I'll see you out there."

I watch him shift into the magnificent gray wolf I remember from that night in the parking lot. The transformation is so elegant, so quick and effortless. I suppose after a hundred years, he should be pretty efficient at it.

He runs off into the woods, leaving me alone in the clearing. Not sure what else to do, I stare up at the moon. I allow its bright glow to fill my vision. I imagine the light reaching inside me, shining in all the shadows. I need to find the wolf inside me. I need to know it's there. I've already experienced the need for blood associated with my vampire side. I need to know my wolf side is also intact.

Something thrums inside me, deep and reverberating like a string on a bass guitar. The vibration fills me, making every part of my body quiver with an energy unlike anything I've felt before. And there's something else—a presence, something fierce and primal. My wolf. I cry out with relief when I feel her. She is inside me, and I want her to come out. I want her to take me over.

As if my consent was all that was needed, something within me begins to change. No, not something—everything. Bones snap and lengthen, and hairs sprout all over my body. A sensation like fire ripples throughout my body, making me whimper. It hurts, yes, but I can handle it.

I drop to all fours, panting. Bile rises in my throat, but I swallow it down. I want this. I accept it. I want my wolf to be free.

And then she is. The human part of my brain is pushed back, my instincts commandeered by the wolf. She knows what to do, where to go, and I trust her. She sniffs the air and follows a familiar scent—campfire. Jack.

The grass is cool and damp with dew under the pads of my paws. As I take off at a run, the ground is soft and inviting.

I run faster than I've ever moved before. My four paws work in concert, not stumbling once. I sense others around me. The forest is alive with movement and sound. A howl erupts on my right, followed almost immediately by several on my left and more in front of me. I tip my head back and add mine to the mix, and even more howls sound in return. My pack is greeting me, accepting me.

I've found my family.

The gray wolf that is Jack bounds through the woods to my side. I can read his face, interpret the joy there. *That was fast,* says a voice in my head. Jack's voice. *First-time shifts usually take longer than that.*

I guess I'm special. I don't expect my thoughts to reach him, but they do.

You'll get used to it, he insists. *As alpha, I can speak to members of the pack in their minds whether they're in human or wolf form, but when we're shifted, we can all speak in each other's minds.*

Cool. It's the only thing I can think to say in response. But I don't want to talk right now; I want to run. Without warning, I take off. *Try to catch me.*

Jack keeps pace with me and the two of us run through the forest. I feel as if I could go faster if I wanted, but I don't see the need. We're just having fun. As we go, others join us before splitting off and going their separate ways. The sensation of running as a wolf is incredible. It's like my whole life I never really lived. Before I thought becoming a were was the mark of my rebirth, but now I know it wasn't. This is.

I may be a hybrid, but I'm a wolf.

I'm not sure how much time has passed when Skye's voice rings through my mind. *Everyone, back to the meeting house to celebrate the successful shift of our newest pack member.*

I join in with the howls that rise up as we all head back to the enclave.

When I make it back to the meeting house, I realize I have no idea how to shift back into human form. But I don't need to—my wolf is still in control. She reverts her dominance over our body back to me, and as her consciousness fades into the background, the fur on my body begins to recede and my bones twist back into their original form. I'm surprised—and pleased—that the pain of shifting is not as acute as it was when I shifted into the wolf. I'm also more than a little shocked to find I'm still clothed. The same jeans and tank top I wore before wolfing out are still in place. I'm not entirely sure how that's possible, but since I don't understand how my body just morphed into a wolf's either, I decide to go with it.

Lillie jogs to my side, back in her human form. "How was it?"

A grin spreads across my face. "Awesome."

She links her arm through mine and guides me up the hill to where the others are gathering. As we go, some of the pack members approach me and congratulate me on my first shift. Others wave and call out from groups dotting the hillside.

I catch a glimpse of Jack as he, Sawyer, and a couple of other guys head into the meeting house. I wonder if they are going to get some food. My stomach growls. All that running left me hungry.

I'm about to head in to see if there's anything I can do to help when someone steps into my path. At first I assume she's simply going to congratulate me as others have done, but when I see her face, my stomach sinks.

Mel.

I haven't seen her since our challenge fight my first night with the pack. I force a smile. "Hey, how's it going?"

Her lip curls back into a snarl. "I told you this wasn't over." She grabs my hand and lifts it straight up. "I challenge Ava to a dominance fight," she yells.

CHAPTER ELEVEN

ALL EYES FLICK in Mel's direction. Skye's eyes flash gold as she steps forward. "Mel, don't be like this."

"I know the rules. I waited until her first shift." Her nails dig into the flesh of my wrist. "I simply want her to prove she really deserves my place in the pack," she growls.

"It's not your place anymore," Lillie says. "She won. She already proved herself."

"What's going on?" Jack calls, emerging from the meeting house. His gaze passes between Mel and me, and he seems to glean the answer himself. His shoulders sag and he sighs before turning toward the rest of the pack. "A challenge has been issued," he calls. "And it will be answered."

Mel smirks as she drops my hand and walks into the center of the circle of bodies that's quickly forming. I turn to Lillie. "What the hell is going on?"

Lillie tugs me toward the outside of the circle. "I knew she was pissed when you took her spot as fourth female, but I never thought she'd do this."

My eyebrows hike upward. "Really? Because she told me she would that first night."

Lillie shakes her head. "I know, but I figured she was all talk. She's always kind of been that way—ever since she joined us." She runs her hands over her hair, smoothing it against her head. "I've heard about other packs where dominance fights happen all the time, but it just doesn't happen here. This isn't the way Jack runs things."

"Then why is he going along with it?"

Lillie sighs. "Because he *has* to. The rules—they're bigger than him. Think of it as werewolf law. If the challenge is issued, it has to be accepted, or Mel could go to the convocation—like, the bosses of all the werewolves. If she goes to them and says Jack isn't obeying pack laws, they could come in and..."

I wait for her to go on. "What? Fire him as alpha?"

She presses her lips together. "Kind of. Only it's not like being alpha is a job. If the convocation sends someone to take over a pack, the alphas—and sometimes the betas, too—are killed."

I swallow. Obviously, refusing to accept Mel's

challenge is out of the question. "So, what? Now I have to fight her again? Why don't I just give her the spot back? I never asked to be the fourth female. I don't care if she takes the title. I'm happy to be the fifth."

She shakes her head. "It's not the way it works. When you and Mel initially fought, you got the best of her, despite the fact that Mel's a better fighter. You'll understand more now that you've shifted, but that night changed the way the pack sees Mel. Our wolves don't believe she's the right one to hold that position anymore. We trust you. If Mel wants the spot, you can't simply give it over. Mel has to prove she's worthy of it."

I run a hand through my hair. "This is nuts." I blow out a breath, trying to formulate a plan. Fine, so I have to fight her. No big deal—I've done that before. I'll just let her win. Then it will be over and I won't have to worry about her holding a grudge, of there being some kind of target on my back.

Jack approaches and Lillie steps away. He puts a hand on each of my shoulders and leans in close. "The rules of a challenge like this dictate that you, as the one being challenged, get to choose which form to fight in."

I'm about to ask for clarification when I realize what he means. I have the choice to stay human or to shift back into a wolf. "What should I do?"

"I think you should stay human because you're far more familiar with this body than your wolf form. But now that you have shifted for the first time, your wolf instincts will have kicked in. Trust them. They'll help you even in this form."

I nod, trying to process all he's telling me.

"This fight isn't going to be like your first one. Unlike that night, when we were just trying to get a sense of where you belong in the pack, the point isn't simply to gauge your abilities. This time, the fight doesn't stop until there's a clear winner."

My jaw drops. "And by clear winner, you mean—"

"It's not a fight to the death," he says grimly. "But something like this usually doesn't end until one of you is incapacitated. Your best bet is to try to knock her out, but if you can't do that, pinning her so she can't gain the upper hand should be enough."

"Should be?" I don't like the sound of that at all.

"Get out here!" Mel shouts from the center of the circle. "This is the girl you chose over me?" she asks the crowd. "She's too afraid to even come start this fight."

Inside me, my wolf's consciousness rears her head. She knows she's being threatened, and she doesn't like it at all. I need to face Mel now before she angers my wolf further.

Only a few yards separate me from Mel when

someone catches my hand and tugs me backward. It's Jack, and he pulls me flush against his body before swooping down to kiss me, hard. My whole body warms, partly with the heat of his kiss, but also with embarrassment at how public this display is. But none of it bothers my wolf. She likes the fact that Jack is claiming me here, now, before the fight, letting everyone know that no matter the outcome, my place with him won't change.

When he releases me he nods, and I turn back toward Mel. Her eyes narrow and she glares at me. I didn't think it was possible for her to be any angrier with me, but my relationship with our alpha seems to have done it.

"I choose to stay human," I say, pleased when my voice sounds sure.

A grin flashes across her face. "I was hoping you'd say that." She lunges toward me and strikes out, hitting my jaw before I can even react. She lands another punch to my stomach and I fall to the ground.

Everything is happening so fast. I can't get my bearings. I try to push myself to my feet, but Mel is there, kicking my sides. I want to curl into a ball to protect myself. I want to yell out to Mel that she's won already, that I can't beat her. No position in the pack is worth this.

But my wolf won't let me. The primal instincts

rise up, and without thinking, I grab for Mel's foot the next time she tries to land a kick. I yank her off balance. She doesn't quite fall, but the reprieve gives me enough time to get to my feet. My eyes prickle, and I'm sure they're flashing gold as I allow my wolf's instincts to take over.

Mel circles me, more cautious now. Her initial attack didn't bring me down, and she needs to be more calculating going forward. When she comes at me again, I manage to block her punches, and I even land one on her jaw. She bounces backward for a moment before rushing me again, and I wind up and aim my fist at her stomach. She doubles over and I back up, giving myself space and time to make a plan.

I need to end the fight. I'm not sure I can knock her out, but I'm pretty sure I can pin her. Mel stands again and I rush her, shoving her to the ground. We tumble one over the other. She was closer to the edge of the hill than I anticipated, and the slope pulls our bodies down. When we finally get to the bottom, we wrestle for the dominant position.

A trickle of blood escapes from the corner of Mel's mouth and a jolt like electricity courses through me. In that instant, I'm able to knock her to the ground and climb on top of her. I straddle her waist and lock my shins over her thighs, pressing her arms down with my hands.

In this position, the red rivulets by her lips catch the moonlight and glisten. I feel a burning in my incisors, the same way I did before I bit Jack, and without thinking, I remove my right hand to cover my mouth.

Mel uses my distraction and swings her arm at my abdomen. But the pain isn't like her earlier punches—this one is a sharp stab, and in an instant I smell my own blood.

A predatory grin spreads itself across Mel's face and she attempts to push me off of her, but I resist. Her expression changes to shock, and she tries to knock me over again. The burning in my mouth subsides as my wolf rises up again. I drop my arm back and punch her hard on the side of the face. Her eyelids flutter for a moment before closing, and her body goes limp.

In the next second, the rest of the pack is rushing down the hill. Jack, Skye, Sawyer, and Dakota lead the way.

"Skye, you and Dakota take care of Mel. She broke the rules of the fight by bringing a knife. Determine an appropriate punishment for her," Jack says.

I spring to my feet and Jack rushes to my side. He brings his lips close to my ear. "Lean on me. Make it look like you're hurt badly."

"What? Why?"

"Do it." His voice is low and almost menacing, and my wolf recognizes his dominance. I shift my weight so I'm depending on him to support me, even though it's unnecessary.

Maggie and Lillie push their way through the crowd until they're at my side. "You can take Ava back to my house," Maggie says. "I'll see to the wound."

"It won't be necessary," Jack says.

The girls exchange confused glances. "But it might need some attention so it heals right," Lillie says cautiously. "There's no one better to look after it than Maggie."

When Jack turns his gaze on them, they shrink back. "I'll take care of her. If I need your help, I'll send for you."

His words settle the matter, and my friends step out of his way as he swings me up into his arms.

I wait until we're nearly to my house to speak. "Jack?"

He shakes his head. "Wait until we're inside."

I do as he says, allowing him to carry me over the threshold and to my room the way he did after bringing me back from the vampires' mansion. He lays me on the bed and lifts my shirt unceremoniously to check the area where Mel stabbed me. I look too. The flesh has already knit itself back together, leaving only what looks like a small scrape.

I glance up at him. "See, I'm okay. I'm fine." But he's still staring at the mark, and I get the sense there's something I'm missing. "This werewolf healing thing is pretty awesome."

My attempt at humor falls flat. Jack doesn't smile when he looks up at me. "It was a silver knife. I've seen Mel use it a thousand times."

A memory clicks into place. My first night, Maggie told me that as a werewolf I'd need to avoid silver. My brow knits with confusion when I look at my nearly healed wound again. "I thought silver was supposed to keep a were from healing quickly like this."

He nods. "It does. There's a thick rubber grip on Mel's knife, because if she touched the silver with her hand, it would burn her skin. It's toxic to weres. That's why she hit you with it. The injury plus the effect of the silver should have weakened you—at least temporarily. Long enough for her to win the fight. But it didn't."

The seriousness of his expression starts to make sense. "Is this because I'm not totally a wolf? Does it have to do with me being part vampire?"

He sighs and settles himself on the mattress beside me. "That's just it—silver has a similar effect on vampires. It's a poison to them just like it is to us."

I try to make sense of what he's telling me. "Then why isn't it having an effect on me?"

"I have no idea." He covers his hand with mine. "I think we need to loop someone else in on what you are."

"Like Lillie?"

He shakes his head. "No, not someone in the pack. Someone I've known many years and trust completely. She may know more about what you are than I do." He runs a hand through his hair. "I was hoping you being a hybrid was something we could deal with on our own, but it looks like things are more complicated. She'll be able to help."

I detect unease in his voice. "You don't sound particularly sure about that."

"I'm not," he admits. "But she's our best shot."

CHAPTER TWELVE

IT'S A TWO-HOUR DRIVE to the small cabin tucked away deep in a thick forest. Jack tells me it wouldn't have taken so long except we had to be sure not to cross into any other alphas' territories. Under normal circumstances, he could reach out to the pack leaders and get their permission to pass through, but these aren't normal circumstances. The fewer people who know where we're going, the better.

I'm nervous when we climb out of the car and approach the house. There's nothing particularly ominous about it. To the contrary, it's rather cheery. Sweet-smelling flowers and herbs line the stone walkway to the porch, and wind chimes made from sea glass tinkle and shine in the sunlight.

My nervousness has everything to do with

who's inside the cabin.

Jack reaches for my hand and squeezes it. "I've told you, there's nothing to worry about."

"I'm about to meet a witch. Sorry if I'm a little apprehensive."

The corner of his mouth quirks upward. "She's not dangerous. You'll like her, I promise."

Before I can respond, the door swings open to reveal a short woman with long, wispy white hair piled on top of her head. She wears an ankle-length patchwork skirt and a bright blue blouse, and she spreads her arms wide in greeting when she sees Jack.

"It's been too long," she says, embracing him.

He returns her hug, lifting her off the ground and eliciting a girlish giggle. "Cassandra," he says as he sets her down, "this is Ava."

She turns her warm brown eyes on me and studies my face as I study hers. Her skin is thin and there are soft laugh lines around her eyes and mouth, but I can't even hazard a guess as to how old she is. Jack told me immortals cannot wield magic, so she must be mortal—but that doesn't help me pinpoint her age. She could as easily be sixty as ninety.

After a moment she extends a hand toward me, and following an encouraging nod from Jack, I take it.

"It's a pleasure to meet you, Ava."

I manage to smile. "It's nice to meet you too, Cassandra."

She takes a step back and waves us toward the house. "I made snacks," she informs us as she leads us toward the door.

Jack doesn't bother hiding his smile. "I expected nothing less." He inhales deeply before releasing a happy sigh. "You didn't."

"Of course I did," she says as she walks toward a small kitchen area.

The cabin is entirely open on the inside. The kitchen is in the far left corner with a dining room area in front of it. In the back right corner is a bed covered in a spread with the same kind of patchwork as Cassandra's skirt. A rocking chair sits in front of a large fireplace directly to my right. The whole place is warm and cheery, but it does nothing to dispel the sense of foreboding in the back of my mind.

Jack pulls out a chair, and it takes me a moment to realize he's done so for me. Once I'm seated, he settles down beside me. "Have you ever had a canelé?" His eyes glint with the excitement of a child on Christmas morning.

"I don't even think I can spell it," I say as Cassandra joins us at the table. She sets down a platter lined with little circular pastries. They smell strongly of vanilla and something spicy I can't quite place.

Jack loses no time scooping one off the plate and biting into it. He closes his eyes and groans softly as he chews. "Do you know how long it's been since I've had one of these?"

Cassandra smiles. "I'm guessing since the last time you came to visit. But I know you didn't just come for my cooking." Her eyes stray to me and I swallow. I didn't ask what kind of powers a witch like Cassandra possesses, but now I wish I would have. Can she read my thoughts? Can she sense my discomfort?

Jack shoves the rest of the pastry into his mouth, giving it a couple of good chews before gulping it down. "No, I didn't." A muscle in his jaw jumps before he continues. "I'm here because I trust you. I need to know what we say here will stay between us."

Her eyebrows hitch upward. "Have I ever given you any reason to question my loyalty?"

He covers her hand with his and squeezes it. "What I'm about to say will test it."

Something passes between them, and I wonder just how long they've known each other. I didn't think to ask Jack how he knows Cassandra or why he's so sure she'll be able—and willing—to help us.

After a moment, Jack removes his hand and

nods toward me. "Ava is newly changed."

Cassandra nods. "I'm not so old I can't tell that."

Jack can't quite hide a smile. "She's not like any other wolf I've ever met."

The corners of Cassandra's mouth quirk upward. "I can tell that, too."

He shakes his head. "It's more than that."

I want to ask him what he means, but he's speaking again before I get the chance.

"This is going to sound crazy—I'm having trouble believing it myself—but the proof is impossible to deny. Somehow she's a hybrid. She's a wolf and a vampire." He leans forward, resting his elbows on the table. "How is that even possible?"

Cassandra holds her hands up. "You need to hold on a minute, Jack. What proof are you talking about? Are you positive?"

Jack glances at me, and I get the feeling he's seeking my permission to tell her everything. I draw back my shoulders and take a breath. "I drank blood. Twice. After I woke up—as a werewolf—I got sick, delirious. I didn't know what I was doing, but I was drawn to a house a vampire was staying in."

"Luke," Jack murmurs.

Cassandra sucks in a breath and stiffens before shaking her head. As she blows out the air, she stretches an arm across the table and covers Jack's hand with hers for an instant. I look from her face to his, searching for any clue as to why Luke's name would elicit such a reaction. It was clear from the conversation between the two men at the mansion that they have a history, but I never asked for any details. I figured the two had run-ins because they live so near each other. Something tells me that's not the whole story.

After a beat, Cassandra turns her wise eyes on me. "Vampires aren't social the way werewolves are. While they often live together in broods of a dozen or so, it's more out of convenience than camaraderie. When they turn someone, it's often on a whim rather than from the desire to make that person family. Still, there's a kind of bond forged when one vampire creates another. Since Luke sired you, you could feel that bond. If you hadn't found him, you might have died before your transition completed."

I think back to the way I felt in Luke's presence. "So I have some sort of bond with him?"

Cassandra presses her lips together. "For their many differences, werewolves and vampires have some similarities. As a pack alpha, Jack's commands are irresistible to the pack members. He didn't create all of them—many follow him by choice. But the power is the same. With vampires, there's no real leader, no hierarchy, except when one vampire turns another."

The idea that Jack or Skye could give an order I would have to obey never struck me as inherently dangerous, but the idea that Luke might have the same kind of power over me makes my stomach twist. "I have to do what Luke says?"

"No," Jack says firmly.

Cassandra holds up her hand as if to silence him. "When you're near him, it will be hard to know what's his will versus yours."

I sigh, relieved. While the explanation is unsettling, at least it explains some things. "That makes sense. When I was with him..." Heat rises in my cheeks as I recall the way I let him kiss me. "It was strange," I say at last.

Cassandra's attention turns back to Jack. "How many others know?"

"I told Skye and Sawyer."

She nods. "Understandable. What about the vampires?"

His lips twitch. "I don't think they knew what she was. Luke seemed genuinely confused about why I'd come for her."

"Let's hope he doesn't get too curious," Cassandra says.

Jack raises his eyebrows. "I think he's proven just how much he cares for anyone other than himself." He crosses his arms over his chest, a shadow passing over his expression. "I don't think he'll be a problem."

I'm doing my best to follow the thread of the conversation, but a question prickles in my mind. "Why is it such a big deal? I get that I'm unique, but why does it matter? Why would anyone care?"

Instead of answering, Cassandra looks at Jack. "I assume you have your reasons. Care to share?"

"Silver doesn't bother her," Jack says quietly. "She's fast—faster than I think she realizes. I got the sense the other night that if she ran full out, no one in the pack would've been able to catch her. And then there's her strength. There was a point during the fight when the power she displayed was more than any wolf or vampire I've ever seen."

Cassandra nods. "And what about the feeding?" She turns her gaze on me. "How often do you need blood?"

I shift, uncomfortable at the question. I don't like how matter-of-fact she is about it, but I suppose that's better than the alternative. I sense in her none of the revulsion the topic brings up for me. "I'm not sure. It's been maybe three days?"

"And how much did you have then?"

I glance down at the table, my stomach lurching. I wasn't exactly paying attention. It's not like I had a measuring cup or anything. After a moment, I make my best guess. "At Luke's, he gave me some. Maybe a cup. And then with Jack..." I pause, catching the way Cassandra jumps with surprise out of the corner of my eye. "I didn't drink much from him. A few mouthfuls, maybe."

"She didn't hurt me," Jack says, and while his words are meant to relieve Cassandra, they make me feel better, too. "It really wasn't that much. She was weak beforehand, but she was better immediately afterward."

"That shouldn't have helped her at all," Cassandra says. "I've never heard of a vampire drinking from a werewolf. I was under the impression they couldn't be sustained that way." She turns her attention back to me. "And you've had no more since then?"

I shake my head. "Why?"

She takes a moment before answering. "Vampires often feed more than they need to survive, of course, but from what I've been told, I'd say your typical vampire would have required more blood than you have so far. I heard the rule of thumb once of a pint to a quart per day."

My nose wrinkles. "I haven't had nearly that much."

"It might be because you're not fully a vampire. You don't need to feed as often, yet you're faster and stronger—and impervious to silver." She stands abruptly and walks back into her kitchen. "I wonder."

"What's she doing?" I whisper to Jack.

He shrugs. "I've learned it's best to just go with it."

When she returns, she carries a clove of garlic and a small glass bottle outfitted with an eyedropper. Jack recoils when she sets the bottle on the table. "Is that really necessary?"

She arches an eyebrow. "We need to know."

I look at the bottle with trepidation. "Know what? What is that?"

"This is garlic," she says, holding it out in her palm.

I fight rolling my eyes. "I know that."

"It's one thing the legends get right. Garlic is like poison to vampires. When applied to the skin, it can burn like acid. I've heard stories of people injecting garlic oil under the skin and in the veins of vampires as a means of torture." She settles back in her chair and stretches her open palm across the table. "I need your hand, please."

After a small nod from Jack, I oblige. "Sunlight won't kill a vampire," she says, adjusting her grip on my hand. "Or make one sparkle," she adds with a wink. "But they're not at full strength in sunlight. That's why so many are active at night." She rubs the clove across the top of my hand. "Do you feel anything?"

The aroma tickles my nose and I can't help smiling. "Besides the desire to dip my hand in some marinara?"

Her eyebrows draw together. "Interesting." She sets the garlic back on the table and picks up the glass bottle. Jack tenses beside me. "Oh, calm down. I won't get any on you."

"What is it?"

"Wolfsbane," he murmurs. "Incredibly toxic to weres. I've had a couple encounters with it in my life, and the pain isn't something I'd wish on my worst enemy." He squints. "Okay, maybe on my worst enemy."

Cassandra shushes him. "I just need to confirm my suspicion." She plucks the dropper from the bottle and brings it to my hand. With practiced fingers, she squeezes out a single bead of liquid.

Just like with the garlic, nothing happens. Besides being aware of the droplet on my skin, I feel nothing. "It's not affecting me. What does that mean?"

"Unfortunately, it means things just got a bit more complicated," Cassandra says, inserting the eyedropper into the bottle and taking it and the garlic back into the kitchen.

The response does nothing to comfort me. "And what does *that* mean?"

"Everything will be fine," Jack says, but

Cassandra talks over him.

"Nature requires equilibrium," she begins as she returns to the table. "As I'm sure you're aware, humans have the tendency to throw that off. Vampires are allowed to exist to keep the human population from getting out of hand. Werewolves exist to keep the vampires from getting out of hand. And witches concern themselves with caring for nature." She sits down heavily in her chair. "Your abilities, your existence, could be seen as a threat to the natural order. We witches don't concern ourselves with the matters of vampires and werewolves much because we know they're not invulnerable. They keep each other in check. But who could keep someone like you in check? If you decided to indulge your vampire side, you might prove too strong for the werewolves to control."

I hold my hands up. "I have no interest in living as a vampire."

"Of that I have no doubt," Cassandra says. "But I'm not the only one who will need convincing. If the werewolves learn what you are, it might make them nervous. You need blood, but according to Jack, you're stronger and faster than a regular were. And you have qualities that would be attractive to a vampire, too. Your imperviousness to silver and garlic—the fact that the sun probably won't affect you the way it affects them. And if the witches learn of you..."

Jack leans forward. "I thought we were keeping this between us."

"And we are. I have no plans to tell my coven. There are those on the council who might see Ava's existence as a sign that the world is worse off than any of us feared. Some already worry that the damage the humans have wrought on the planet can't be reversed. I doubt the news of a new hybrid will be well received."

I glance between Jack and Cassandra. "Wait—a new one? From how Jack was talking, I sort of assumed I was the only one."

"You are," Cassandra says. "As far as I know, you're the only one since the first."

It's Jack's turn to be confused. "The first? What are you talking about?"

She sighs. "After all these years, you have no idea how your kind came to be?" She swats his arm playfully before going on. "As the legend goes, there was once a witch named Ulrich who gave up his connection to nature, to magic, to turn himself into something he considered stronger and more powerful. He was the father of all the vampires and werewolves—the first hybrid. When the witches of his day realized the danger such a creature posed, they knew they had to stop him. They couldn't undo his magic and were unwilling to kill him for fear of darkening their souls, so they devised a means to split him—his soul—into two bodies: the wolf and the vampire. They figured his evil could serve the greater good and help with the balance, leaving the witches to deal exclusively with the protection of the natural world."

Her story sounds crazy. How could it be possible? Then again, what could be impossible, given what I've been through in the last week? Of all the questions spinning in my mind, one gets the best of me: "How did they split his soul? I mean, how is it possible to live with only half a soul?"

Cassandra glances at Jack, a puzzled expression flickering across her face. "Immortality goes against nature. Everything is supposed to be born, live, and die. To keep balance, once a person becomes an immortal—through being turned or through birth, in the case of some werewolves—half their soul splits off. That piece is later born inside another body."

I still don't get what she's saying. "Like twins?"

She shakes her head. "No, not a person's twin—their counterpart. Their other half."

I bring my hand to my chest. Can it be true? Did half of my soul split off when I turned? "How could I have not noticed that?" I ask, more to myself than anyone in particular. "Maybe it's because everything changed so quickly—or because I was so close to death. It seems like something I should've realized, though."

Cassandra's eyebrows draw together. She studies me for a moment before giving a heavy sigh and turning to Jack. "You haven't told her?"

Jack straightens, visibly riled. "It hasn't exactly come up," he growls.

"Told me what?" I can understand Jack not wanting to sit me down and explain how my rebirth as a werewolf came with a price. How on earth would one even begin a conversation about losing a piece of your soul?

Cassandra narrows her eyes at Jack before her expression softens and she leans across the table toward me. "Your soul didn't split when you were changed. You were born a half."

I stare at her, trying to make sense of what she's saying. "But I was human. How could I only have half a soul?"

"Oh, sweetheart, you have a whole soul—it's simply split across two bodies. If you choose to merge with your other half, you will have access to abilities beyond what you have now. These are natural inclinations that will be strengthened by the magic that originally created your kind."

The more she explains, the less things make sense. "If witches made it so immortals couldn't have whole souls, why would they allow an immortal to have special powers when they merge with their other half? It kind of seems to defeat the purpose."

She smiles kindly. "It does, until you know the price. If you choose to merge, it's not just your soul that's connected, it's your life force. Once merged, if your other half dies, you'll die too. Balance."

"Finding your half is very rare," Jack says, his eyes trained on the table. "The person who houses the other half of your soul can be born anywhere, anytime. Vampires couldn't care less about finding their halves. Like Cassandra said, they don't thrive in a family like weres do. Then there are the truly selfish ones who kill their halves before they can merge to make sure nothing makes them vulnerable to dying. Wolves, on the other hand, see merging as the greatest blessing they can receive. I've known a few merged couples, and they don't consider it a curse to be destined to die with their halves because they can't imagine living without them."

The desire in Jack's tone is palpable. It's obvious he longs to feel a connection that strong. I feel foolish. I was beginning to think Jack might actually like me, but it seems I'm nothing more than fresh meat to him—a conquest to be had while he waits for his soulmate. I can't keep the bitterness from my voice when I speak. "So I take it you'll merge with your half if you ever find her."

He shifts in his seat, not raising his eyes.

Is he ashamed that I've found out his intentions with me? I glance at Cassandra, hoping to be able to read something in her face. She seems like a kind woman, and I can't see her condoning this kind of behavior. But when I meet her eyes, her expression is serious. "Tell me, Ava. The night you were changed, did Jack bite you?"

"What? No." I shake my head emphatically. "Luke bit me, not Jack."

She nods as if she expected the answer. "Have you stopped to consider why you became a hybrid, not a vampire?"

My mind struggles to process her words. "Of course I have, but..." I shake my head, still not sure what she's getting at.

"As I said, you were born a half. It means your soul is already tethered to the supernatural world. It's always been in you to become a wolf—under the right circumstances."

"I was going to bite you," Jack murmurs. "But before I could, I saw that you were changing. I've seen the transition from human to were so many times it was obvious. I'd heard stories of halves spontaneously turning, but I figured they were fantasy—werewolf romance stories." He shakes his head, not meeting my eyes. "That night wasn't the first time I'd seen you. I noticed you around town months ago, and I felt this...tug. But it never even dawned on me to hope..."

I wait for him to continue, but he seems unable to put the rest of his thoughts into words. I glance at Cassandra, hoping she can shed some light on the situation.

Her eyes are soft, and a smile crinkles the skin around her mouth. "Sweetheart, haven't you figured it out? It's clear to anyone with eyes that you care for him, but now you're worried that his feelings for you aren't as deep—that he'll abandon you if ever he finds his half. What you're not realizing is he's already found his half. It's you."

CHAPTER THIRTEEN

WE DON'T SPEAK on the car ride back to the enclave. Neither of us has said a word to the other since Cassandra dropped the bomb about me being Jack's half. There are so many thoughts twisting in my mind, I'm not sure which I should say first. I keep waiting for Jack to explain, but after more than an hour of silence, I need answers.

"It's why you were in the parking lot that night, isn't it?"

He's quiet for so long afterward, I'm convinced he's not going to respond.

"Yes. After the first time I saw you, I tried to stay away, but I couldn't. Whenever I could get away from the enclave, from my duties, I'd go to town to catch a glimpse of you." He swallows, his Adam's apple bobbing. "But that night, I wasn't out looking for you. There were reports of some new vampires passing through town and I was out on watch. I didn't even expect to see you because you usually left the bar by eleven."

I don't know how I feel knowing that Jack has been watching me. "If you knew we were connected, why didn't you approach me?"

"And say what? I'm the werewolf other half of your soul? I'm sure that would've gone over well."

I press my lips into a tight line. He's right, of course. I would've thought he was crazy. And if he'd simply approached me like any other guy, I probably would've blown him off. But that doesn't answer everything. "How could you have known I was your half before you met me?"

"I can't explain it."

"Try," I snap. It strikes me that I probably shouldn't take such a tone with my alpha, but I can't help myself.

After a few moments, he turns to look at me. "You can't feel it?" His eyes go back to the road. "There's something about you that draws me in, that makes me want to be close to you. I guess I figured you felt it too."

My stomach clenches. Of course I've had that feeling. I've been drawn to Jack since I met him—but I'd convinced myself it was a consequence of him being my alpha. I never considered it was something far deeper. An idea crosses my mind that makes panic rise in my chest. "Does the rest of the pack know?" I don't like the idea of being the last one to find out something so massive. I'm afraid they'll all expect something from me because of it, and it's too much pressure.

"Skye, Sawyer, and Dakota know. And Mel."

I curse. "Why would you tell Mel?"

"Believe me, I wish I hadn't, given everything that's happened. I wanted Skye and the betas to know because I wasn't sure what kind of power shift would happen, or how your presence would change the pack dynamics. And Mel... She was in the right place at the right time. I figured it wouldn't hurt if the fourth female knew—plus, she was curious about why I was asking her and Lillie to watch over your transition in your apartment."

I raise my eyebrows. "Is that not usually how things go?"

He shakes his head. "Under normal circumstances, the were who turns someone takes that person back to his pack. But you were different. I didn't actually turn you—not in the traditional way. And I... I wanted to let you choose to join us. Me."

Part of me wants to be mad about this whole situation—about the fact that Jack has known something so important about me for so long and not bothered to mention it. But I can tell from the tone of his voice that he's just as confused about how to navigate this situation as I am. "What does it even mean that I'm your half? Where do we go from here?"

"It's as much up to you as it is to me," he says, his tone gentle. "I'm just as much your half as you are mine."

I consider this. I suppose it makes sense. Cassandra didn't say anything about one part of the soul having more claim than the other. What was the word she used? Counterpart. One of the questions that's been nagging me bubbles to the surface. "How does merging work?" The next part of the question makes a blush rises in my cheeks, but I need to know. "Is it like... marriage?" The word feels strange in my mouth. I'm nineteen. None of my romantic relationships up until now have been particularly serious. I guess I've always thought marriage would be in the cards for me, but it's always been something nebulous, something that might happen one day.

"Yes and no," he says. "There's no special ceremony, no legal forms—and there's no going back. Once halves merge, their life force is one. I've only known a handful of merged couples. The connection is hard to describe. After the merging, they really seem to become two parts of the same whole. I've never seen people so in love."

The word takes me off guard. Love? How can I be expected to love Jack? I've only just met him. Still, the connection I feel to him can't be denied. I haven't felt this secure in any relationship since my father died. He's told me again and again he'll keep me safe, and I haven't doubted it for an instant. But feeling a connection and committing to someone for life are two different things. "I'm not ready for this."

Jack turns the car, and I recognize the scent and feel of the enclave. I've been so distracted, I didn't notice how close we were. He drives slowly along the loop that takes us through the settlement and parks the car near our houses. My hand goes to undo the seatbelt, but Jack covers it with his. "Luckily, you have all the time in the world. That's the benefit of immortality."

I smile. He's right, of course. Jack has been patient with me thus far, and I don't see that changing now that I know the nature of our connection. He's waited more than a century to find me. A little more time won't hurt anything.

I climb out of the car, wondering if Lillie is in the house and whether I should tell her about being Jack's half, but before I can take more than a few steps, my skin prickles. Something's wrong.

A glance in Jack's direction reveals he senses

the same thing. “Invaders.” He takes a deep breath through his nose. “There are wolves encroaching on our territory.”

I don’t need to be told this is a bad thing. Jack shifts and runs for the woods, and I’m on his heels. Even though it’s only my second time doing it, the transformation is faster than before, and the pain isn’t as acute.

We join with other members of the pack a little way in. It seems we’ve all sensed the intrusion. I wonder how often something like this happens, but probably isn’t the time to ask.

Their scent is strong now, and I know the foreign wolves are near before I see them. Skye approaches them and shifts back to human form. Jack, Dakota and Sawyer step forward as well. Cecily, the third female, edges toward the front of the pack, along with the third and fourth males. It strikes me I should probably do the same, but before I can move, Jack sends a thought to me: *Stay back with Lillie. We don’t know why they’re here, and you’re still new at this.*

A low growl escapes my lips. My wolf doesn’t like being told to stand down, but she respects Jack’s authority and complies. I glance around and find Lillie a few paces behind me. It’s odd how certain I am it’s her, even in her wolf form. I’m not entirely sure how to send a thought message to her, but we lock eyes and I give it a try. *What's going on?*

This pack has tried to move in on our territory before, but they've never been able to get a foothold, she replies. *Most wolves respect each other's boundaries, but not Justin and Chrissy. And they fight dirty.*

But what are they doing here now? I wonder.

Jack moves to Skye's side and transforms back into a human as well. Two wolves from the invading pack step forward and do the same. I assume the girl with the wild blonde hair and the guy with shifty eyes are Chrissy and Justin.

I glance back at Lillie. *Why are they shifting?*

We can only communicate with other members of our pack while in wolf form.

"We demand an audience," Chrissy snarls.

"This isn't how things are done," Skye says. "You don't just arrive unannounced and demand to speak with another pack's alphas. There are protocols for this kind of thing."

"And what's the protocol for werewolves aligning with vampires?" Justin demands. "Don't try to lie and tell us there's not one among you. Two in our pack are halves, and they're extra sensitive to vampires. We know every time a leech is turned in a hundred-mile radius."

"Good for you," Jack says, his tone dismissive. "I can assure you we're not allying ourselves with vampires."

Another wolf steps forward and shifts to human. Her build is slight and her dark hair is styled in a spiky pixie cut. "I know there's one here—nearby."

My stomach sinks. Can this wolf really sense me? What if she points me out? What will the rest of my pack do?

"Do you now?" Skye asks, her tone condescending. "And what do you imagine we'd be doing with a vampire in our territory?"

"We don't know," Chrissy says, an edge to her voice. "But Sara says this vampire's energy is different than anything she's ever felt before."

Jack crosses his arms over his chest. "Even if we had a hundred vampires camped out in our territory, it would be of no consequence to you."

An expression flickers over Sara's face and she darts to Chrissy's side before whispering something in her alpha's ear. Chrissy's response is quiet, but the movement of her lips makes her words clear: *Are you sure?* When Sara nods, Chrissy lifts her chin imperiously.

Sara takes her cue. I know what's about to happen a split second before she lifts her hand to point directly at me. "That wolf is part vampire."

Surprise ripples through my pack. It's strange being able to sense the emotions of so many others at once. I have the feeling many of them want to look at me, but only Lillie and Maggie do.

"Do you deny it?" Justin asks.

"No." There's no hesitation in Jack's voice.

A handful of members from the invading pack howl, causing my fur to stand on end. A few of them step forward as if waiting on an order to attack.

"How can you stand by and allow this abomination to live?" Chrissy asks. "I know your reputation, Jack. You've never been soft when leeches are involved."

"She is a wolf first," Jack growls. "And she is under my protection."

"Your protection," Chrissy scoffs. "And who's supposed to protect the rest of us from *her*?"

"She's not a threat to you," Skye snaps.

"Maybe not yet," Justin insists. "But what happens when she makes more like herself? Who could control a pack of hybrids?"

I can't keep silent any longer. I know Jack and Skye want to speak for me, to protect me, but I can stand up for myself. I shift back into human form and take a few steps forward. Half of the invaders recoil. "I have no intention of making more hybrids. I don't even know how. I don't want to cause any trouble."

Justin glares, his eyes full of malice. "You already have."

In a flash, Justin, Chrissy, and Sara shift back into their wolves and the invaders attack. Panic floods me. I'm frozen. The flurry of movement and the chorus of growls and snarls make me forget the new strength and imperviousness of my body. I feel small, vulnerable.

Until my wolf takes over. She overwhelms my senses and I shift without a thought. I allow her instincts to take control as a wolf with a brown coat runs toward me. I move out of the way at the last second and swipe at the would-be attacker as she passes. She spins and bares her teeth, and I snarl before lunging for her.

After a couple tries, I manage to knock her over. Before she can recover, I'm on top of her, biting down on her neck. My plan is simply to hold her down, to wait for the other pack to call for a retreat, but one of my teeth slices along the flesh beneath her fur. My lip curls at the aroma—this blood won't do, it won't satisfy—but I still want it. I want to rip out this wolf's neck and lap her blood with my tongue.

Horrified, I unclamp my mouth and take a step back. No. I can't—I *won't.* But I want to. The vampire part of me doesn't care that there's a battle going on—she wants to feed. I fight the urge but I'm afraid to move, afraid of what might happen if I do.

The one I had pinned before rises to her paws

and is joined by a snow-white wolf. Chrissy. I'm outnumbered. I should run, but my muscles are frozen.

Chrissy and the other wolf leap at me, but before they can make contact, Skye rockets into their flanks, knocking them off course. She and the brown wolf roll on the ground until Skye manages the dominant position. She clamps her mouth around her neck and shakes until the brown wolf's head breaks loose from her body. I watch, revulsion and longing mingling in my stomach.

Chrissy takes advantage of my distraction and leaps on top of me. She scratches my back and I howl in pain, but before she can do any more damage, Skye rams her until she topples off me.

A baying cry rends the air. Justin. He's calling for a retreat. All around, members of his pack run toward our border. But not Chrissy. Her body lengthens as she shifts back into human form. I can't figure out why she would do that, until she shoves her hand into Skye's ribcage.

A howl rips itself from my throat as Chrissy pulls Skye's heart from her chest. She pushes Skye's limp body off her and stands, a look of gruesome satisfaction on her face. "Let that be a warning to you and your wolves, Jack! There are consequences for allying yourself with such a monster."

She takes off at a run and I give chase. She's still

in human form; I could easily outstrip her, but a voice booms in my head. *No. Don't go after her.*

I turn to see Jack staring right at me. *Why? Didn't you see what she did?*

His head drops. *Yes. But retaliation won't bring Skye back.* He turns to address the rest of the pack. *I know you have many questions, and I plan to answer them all, but not now. First, join me at the meeting house to mourn the loss of Skye and to celebrate her life.*

After a beat, Lillie howls, followed by Maggie. Sawyer joins next. One by one, each member of the pack joins in. It's a sound of unspeakable sadness.

CHAPTER FOURTEEN

I'M ON HIGH ALERT as soon as my eyes snap open the next morning.

I'm not in my room.

It's not until I sit up and take in my surroundings that the adrenaline in my system begins to ebb. Fuzzy recollections from last night stitch themselves together in my mind.

After we buried Skye, the pack congregated in the field behind the meeting house. Jack and a few others built a bonfire like the one that burned the night I joined the pack. Person after person came forward to share something about Skye. When everyone who wanted to speak was given the opportunity, Jack officially named Dakota as the new alpha female, and Cecily as the beta.

While there was no fanfare around it, their

promotions mean I'm now the third female. And Mel is back to her spot as fourth.

Sawyer insisted the eight highest-ranking weres do shots of Skye's favorite liquor in her honor. I stopped after three, and things devolved into a kind of alcoholic anarchy. By the time Jack announced everyone should head back to their houses to rest and prepare for some necessary changes that would be implemented in the morning, Lillie was so drunk she could hardly walk in a straight line. When we finally made it home—after I carried her about half of the way—she begged me to stay with her until she fell asleep.

I must've fallen asleep too.

Lillie stirs beside me. She blinks a few times and squints at me before dropping her gaze. "It wasn't a bad dream, was it?"

I struggle to swallow around the rapidly-forming lump in my throat. "I'm afraid not."

She sits up. After all the shots she drank last night, I expect her to sway or to clutch her head, but she does neither. Do werewolves not get hangovers? "I... I guess I should take a shower. We'll probably need to increase security around the territory's perimeter today, so..." She doesn't quite look at me as she speaks.

The heavy weight of guilt settles in my stomach. "You cared about Skye a lot, didn't you?"

Lillie takes in a breath before turning her brown eyes on me. "She's been the alpha female since about a decade after I joined the pack. She was fierce, but kind. I trusted her completely."

The description only makes me feel worse. "It's my fault she's gone."

Lillie puts a hand on my shoulder. "Don't think like that. She died protecting you because that was her responsibility. Our alphas are our leaders, sure, but they're also our greatest defenders. I trust Jack with my life because I know he would give his to keep me safe. And even though it's Dakota's first day as alpha, I know the same is true of her. And, for what it's worth, I know it's true of you, too."

Tears prickle my eyes and I pull Lillie in for a hug. It's exactly what I needed to hear. Not only does she not blame me for Skye's death, the revelation that I'm half vampire hasn't shaken her faith in me. I squeeze her tightly, wishing I knew how to express how much she's come to mean to me in the last week.

Some of the tension that's built in my shoulders is just beginning to ebb when a scent in the air makes me stiffen up again. My skin is tingling like it did yesterday when Jack and I sensed the invading pack. But this is different. There's something familiar in the scent, but I can't place it.

A knock sounds at the front of the house and I

separate from Lillie before jogging out of her room. My breath catches as I open the door. Jack. How is it possible that he's even more attractive today than ever before? Is it the sunlight that makes him glow like something otherworldly, or is it due to what I learned yesterday about our connection—about us sharing one soul?

"We have a visitor," he says by way of greeting. "She'll be at my place in a few minutes."

I understand the invitation implicit in his words and step out onto the porch. The back of his hand brushes mine as we start toward his house. The scent of the intruder is stronger now, and I'm able to place it. "It's Cassandra, isn't it?"

He smiles down at me. "Very good. When did you first sense her?"

"Just before you knocked."

He nods as we approach his door. He opens it and allows me to enter before him. "Your ability to feel when someone crosses into our territory will continue to improve. I'm actually impressed. It took Sawyer far longer to be able to sense intrusions."

We step up onto his porch and he reaches for the doorknob, but before he can twist it, I tug on his arm until he turns to me. We didn't get to talk much last night. He was too busy comforting the others, and I felt their need for reassurance was greater than mine for absolution. "I'm so sorry about Skye.

I froze, and—"

He shakes his head and cradles my face in his palms. "Skye was a good alpha, and she'll be missed. But if she hadn't stepped in when she did..."

My heart twists. "I get it. I'm your half. If I died, you would've too."

His brow furrows and he shakes his head. "We're not merged. If you'd died last night, I'd still be alive—at least, I'd still be here." He leans down and presses a hard kiss to my lips. The force is dizzying, and I'm glad for his hands holding me up. "I just found you." His eyes smolder as they study my face, the intensity overwhelming. No one has ever looked at me like that, and I'm not entirely sure what to make of it. The emotion radiating off him is enough to make my breath catch. And there's something rising inside me, something almost primal. I wish I hadn't stopped him before we got into the house—I wish we weren't standing on his porch right now. I want him to kiss me again, and I don't want him to stop.

A car door slams, invading the moment. Jack breaks eye contact and I take in a deep breath.

Cassandra's expression indicates she understands she's interrupted something between us, and her gaze is apologetic as she starts up the hill.

Jack pushes open the door, and I cross the

threshold. By the time I've taken a spot on the couch, Cassandra is inside. Jack closes the door behind him and takes a seat beside me. When Cassandra sits on the adjacent loveseat, she gives a heavy sigh. "Jack called me last night to tell me what happened, and I spent several hours scrying to get a sense of how many others know about what you are. The news isn't good."

Jack curses under his breath. "Did Justin's pack spread the word?"

Cassandra nods. "I don't think they were too pleased with their defeat, so they decided the best way to get back at you was to tell everyone they know about Ava."

I do my best to follow the conversation. I assume scrying must be some kind of witch way of learning things. There was a girl I knew in middle school who claimed to be clairvoyant—able to sense things happening in other locations. As a witch, I don't doubt Cassandra would be capable of something like that. "So, more people know what I am. What does it mean?"

Cassandra presses her lips together. "You're not safe. Even the witches have caught wind of what's happening, and the council is meeting later this afternoon to determine what steps—if any—we need to take to ensure Ava's existence poses no threat."

Jack growls, his eyes flashing gold.

Cassandra holds up her hand. "*Calme-toi, Jacques.*"

I look from Cassandra to Jack and back again. Was that French? Lillie once told me Jack's father was French, but why would Cassandra speak that language to him? Before I can ask, Cassandra is talking again.

"They've asked for Ava to be present, and I think it's a good idea." She leans forward, resting her forearms on her thighs. "I'm going to do all I can to convince the council Ava poses no threat and has no plans to create more hybrids. My word carries weight, but I'm not sure it'll be enough. With your consent, I'll tell them the two of you are halves."

"Why do they need to know that?" I ask, too quickly. Hurt flashes in Jack's eyes, and a pang of guilt shoots through me. I didn't mean to sound so defensive about it. I'm just starting to wrap my head around the whole idea myself. I'm not sure I want everybody knowing about our connection just yet.

"Being Jack's half allies you more closely with the wolves than vampires, which will cast you in a positive light," Cassandra says, her tone easy despite the fact the tension in the room is palpable. "And Jack's history of keeping local vampires in check is well known, which, again, could help the council determine your existence won't cause any harm."

I swallow. "Let's play it by ear. If it looks like telling them will help things, do it."

She holds my gaze. "And if they ask you to merge?"

Jack crosses his arms over his chest. "Why would they demand that? They understand what it means, don't they? Would they really press to take Ava's free will out of the matter?"

Cassandra sighs, regarding him the way a mother would look at a child throwing a tantrum. "I'm not saying they *will* ask you to, I'm simply suggesting they *may*. Her strengths and invulnerabilities will likely make some on the council nervous. Merging would at least take immortality off the table."

"What a beautiful reason to choose to merge," Jack mutters darkly.

I chew on my lower lip. Cassandra's point makes sense, but it doesn't make the idea any easier to swallow. What I told Jack before is still true: I'm not ready. Merging now simply to make the witches feel better about my existence sounds about as appealing as an arranged marriage to a stranger.

Jack sighs. "Thanks for letting us know what's going on. Now we can be prepared for the meeting tonight."

Cassandra stands, understanding she's been

dismissed. But instead of heading to the door, she brushes past Jack, slowing as she approaches me. She wraps her arms around me. I'm surprised by the embrace, but also pleased. She trusts Jack, and by extension, she trusts me. I have no doubt she will do everything in her power to plead my case to the other witches tonight.

Once she releases me, she squeezes Jack's arm before letting herself out.

It's not until I hear her car pull away that I look at Jack. "Thanks for standing up for me."

"Always." Jack sighs and collapses down onto the loveseat Cassandra had been occupying. He pats the spot beside him but doesn't speak until I sit. "So you know, when the time comes that you want to merge—*if* it comes—I'm ready. I'm prepared for what it would mean to merge, and I don't want to force you into something you're not ready for just because you think you have to. I don't want you to make this decision because Cassandra says it would be best, or because you're afraid. Circumstances shouldn't force your hand. I want it to be your choice." He locks his eyes on mine. "*I* want to be your choice."

I don't know how to respond. I want to tell him something to make him feel better. I want him to know how much he's grown to mean to me in such a short time. I want to express how part of me yearns for him, but I don't know how to put it in words.

He stands. "I need to meet with Mel. Pack law dictates that, as the fourth female, she's among the highest ranking weres in the pack. But I need to know I can trust her. Sawyer is waiting in the gym for you to do some training. I know you've been working with Lillie, but I think he'll probably be a better teacher."

I nod. I wish we didn't have these responsibilities to tend to. I really do want to talk about the prospect of merging and what it would mean, but now is not the time. "We'll talk later?"

In response, he leans down to kiss me. Tingles of electricity dance along my nerve endings. "No matter what the witches say, you always have a place in this pack, and at my side."

His words seem to sink in through my skin, warming me and making me feel at peace despite the threats surrounding me. I hope the witches realize I'm not a threat, but it's comforting to know Jack will be with me no matter what.

CHAPTER FIFTEEN

WITH EACH MILE Jack takes us closer to the witches' council meeting, the knot in my stomach grows tighter. It started when I was training earlier with Sawyer. He knocked me on my ass so much it was embarrassing, but I was distracted by thoughts of what might happen tonight. Jack has assured me time and again that in all his dealings with witches over the decades, they've proven themselves to be fair. They don't seek out violence. They tend toward harmony among living things. And Cassandra was too modest when she spoke of her influence on the council—she's been the leader for longer than I've been alive. Still, I can't help noticing how Jack's muscles are coiled, like he's ready to spring into action at the slightest provocation.

The cabin Jack parks in front of is larger than

the one where Cassandra lives, but it has the same kind of natural beauty, like it sprang up organically from the surrounding forest. Cassandra greets us at the door, but she doesn't smile as she ushers us in. The cabin is lit by candles, even though the sun won't set for several hours. Nestled in the woods the way it is, not much sunlight filters in through the windows. The whole vibe of the place makes me think of a field trip I took in elementary school to Greenfield Village—an outdoor museum filled with historic structures that gave me the feeling I'd been transported back in time. I wouldn't be surprised if someone were baking bread from scratch or churning butter in a corner.

The room is dominated by a large, oval table, around which six people are seated. Half of them appear to be as old as Cassandra—however old that may be—while two more appear to be in their late thirties or early forties. A woman with dark red hair, who sits at the head of the table, appears to be the youngest one present—maybe in her twenties. But again, I have no idea how witches age, so maybe she's much older.

Cassandra leads us to the end of the table opposite the red-haired woman. She takes a seat and indicates we should sit in the smaller chairs to her right and left. I feel the weight of everyone's gaze on me, and I do my best not to shrink under it.

I don't want to give them the impression that I have anything to be ashamed of here. For his part, Jack looks entirely confident, but his jaw is clenched even as he attempts to smile at the council members.

The red-haired woman stands and draws back her shoulders. Her sharp emerald-green eyes study me shrewdly. "My name is Kiara, and it falls to me to lead this meeting. I won't lie: The council is somewhat disturbed by reports of what you are, Ava."

It shouldn't surprise me that she knows my name, but the syllables send an electric jolt down my spine. "That I'm a hybrid, you mean."

She nods. "You don't deny it?"

My gaze flickers to Jack before I answer. "I don't plan to lie to you today. I won't deny I'm a hybrid because that's what I've been told I am."

"Is it true silver doesn't poison you the way it does a were or a vampire?" she asks.

"Yes," I say. My throat is dry, and I wish there were a glass of water somewhere.

"And you aren't consumed by bloodlust the way a vampire is?" she continues.

My stomach lurches as I remember the intense swells of desire I've experienced in the presence of blood. Even though I know werewolf blood can't sustain me, seeing it, smelling it, has been enough to make my teeth lengthen. I don't know how I would respond if I were near a human who was bleeding, and I don't want to find out. "I don't need to feed as often," I say after a beat. It's not exactly an answer to her question, but it's the closest thing I know for sure.

Kiara's thin eyebrows arch. "And where does your allegiance lie?"

I take in a breath, relieved that she's gotten to this question so early. I nod at Jack. "I consider myself a werewolf. I'm a member of Jack's pack."

There's a subtle shift in the atmosphere as the five members between Cassandra and Kiara seem to let out a collective breath. My words have put many of them at ease. A woman with salt-and-pepper hair pulled back into a long braid sighs as tension visibly drains from her shoulders.

But Kiara doesn't sit down. "And what is your role in the pack?"

I glance at Jack before turning to Cassandra, but she doesn't look at either of us. Her eyes are trained on Kiara. "I'm new," I begin tentatively, "so I'm still learning what it means to be a werewolf."

Kiara's full lips curve into a smile. "But packs are split by a hierarchy of sorts, are they not? There are more submissive wolves and their pack leaders—the alphas and betas. Where do you fall on the continuum?"

The unease that had begun to unravel in my stomach coils itself once more. For the first time since learning where I stand in the pack, I wish I were more submissive—more like Lillie or Maggie. I could make it seem as if I am, but I don't think it's in my best interest to attempt to deceive anyone. "I'm the fourth female. Third, I mean."

If my last answer served to comfort the council, this one has only upset it again. Unease ripples through those seated around the table. Besides Cassandra, the only one who seems unsurprised by this news is Kiara.

"You don't sound entirely confident," she says.

There's something in her tone I don't like. "It's new. Our alpha female was killed last night, so my place in the pack changed."

Kiara tilts her head. "I understand. Pack hierarchies are hardly written in stone. The death of someone who ranks higher than you can effect your status. And there are always dominance fights."

My wolf bristles at her insinuation. "I have no desire to challenge anyone to a fight for dominance."

"But you could," says the woman with salt-and-pepper hair.

Jack leans forward. "What does this have to do with anything?"

Kiara's lips curve into a smile when she looks at

him. “The alpha speaks. Good, I’d like to clarify something. Is it true that an alpha’s orders must be obeyed by pack members?”

“Yes,” he says, his voice tight. He’s doing his best to keep his expression impassive, but I catch a steely glint in his eye.

Kiara continues. “What would happen if you were to command your pack members to submit to becoming hybrids?”

“I’d like to think my history with vampires would be enough to assure you I’d never do that,” Jack growls.

If Kiara is bothered by his tone, her expression doesn’t show it. “And what if pack dynamics shift again? What if Ava becomes alpha female and decides to give the order herself?”

“I would never let that happen,” Jack says, his voice low and dangerous.

Kiara narrows her eyes. “How far would you go to stop her? Once an alpha’s command is given, there’s no way to keep it from being carried out—unless the one who spoke it gives the counter commands. I’m under the impression that one alpha can’t command another, so you wouldn’t be able to order her to do that. If that’s true, the only way to keep such a command from being carried out would be to kill its issuer. Forgive me, but I find it hard to believe if it came down to it, you’d be willing to kill your half."

The word hits me like a bucket of ice water. I turn to Cassandra, a sense of betrayal building in me at the idea that she would have told the council before we even arrived, but she looks just as surprised by Kiara's revelation as we are.

The gazes of the witches at the table are now distrustful. A man with close-cropped black hair and a graying goatee turns an accusatory eye on Cassandra. "You said she posed no threat. You claimed we were seeing portends where there were none, that the world hadn't fallen too far out of balance—that the earth could still be saved. But you can't tell me this girl's existence isn't an omen. The scales have tipped—this world is beyond salvation."

Cassandra's face remains calm. "Stephen, listen to yourself. You are allowing unfounded accusations to—"

"We all know you have a... special connection with the werewolf," Kiara says. "It seems you're the one whose judgment is clouded. You'd rather allow the world to end than betray your pet. You are no longer of one mind with the council." She draws her shoulders back, a satisfied smirk playing at the corners of her mouth. "You are removed as our head. Now, on my authority, take the hybrid into custody."

Panic sweeps through me as the council

members stand to obey Kiara's command. To get to the front door, I need to go around the table—or over it. But if I were to jump, it's likely one of the witches would grab me before I made it to the other side. There's a small window directly behind me, but it's too high to jump through easily.

"Get down," Cassandra hisses. Without waiting for an explanation, Jack and I hit the floor. A split second later, energy pulses from Cassandra's fingertips and the witches are knocked backward. As they hit the ground, Jack shifts. I follow suit and chase him to the large, low picture window at the front of the house. Without hesitating, Jack jumps through it, shattering the glass. He hits the porch outside and doesn't miss a beat. When I jump through, jagged shards dig into my paws, but I ignore the pain and run into the woods after Jack. We are only a few yards into the trees when I glance over my shoulder and whine. Cassandra isn't following us.

We need to leave, Jack insists. *It's what Cassandra would want. The witches won't kill her—it's not their way. We'll come back later with reinforcements and get her out.*

As much as I don't want to go, I know Jack is right. I block out the pain in my paws as we run over roots, moss, and fallen twigs. What's important now is putting distance between us and the witches.

I was right to dread this meeting. But the worst thing is, I'm not the only one who's affected by the outcome. As I run, all I can do is hold onto hope that Jack is right about the witches not harming Cassandra. I don't know if I'll be able to forgive myself if someone else dies trying to protect me.

CHAPTER SIXTEEN

THE WEAKNESS comes over me so quickly I nearly fall on my snout as we enter our territory. I wonder if it's adrenaline that's kept me going this long. The familiar burning ignites in my stomach, and I stop and shift back to human form.

When Jack senses what I've done, he shifts too. "What's wrong?"

I turn my attention to my hands. Small flecks of glass sparkle in the light coming through the tree branches, and I use my nails to start digging it out. I don't want to tell him what's really going on, but I also don't want to lie, so I hope my actions lead him to his own conclusions.

After a moment, he takes my hand in his and starts digging the glass out for me. I take deep breaths, trying to focus on the pain to keep my mind off the pangs of hunger. "You know, if we keep running we'll be at the enclave in five minutes. We could take care of this there."

The idea of running any further makes me want to faint. "It's not that."

He runs the pads of his thumbs over my palms. As I watch, the small holes left by the shards of glass mend themselves. "What is it then?"

I sigh. "I'm hungry," I say, not meeting his eyes. "I mean, part of me is."

A beat passes before he inhales with understanding. "Oh."

And just like that, things are awkward. Of course Jack is aware of my vampire side, but mostly we can ignore it. Now, here it is, rearing its head.

"Could you... Would..." He exhales noisily and his lips twitch like he's trying to figure out exactly the right words. "Could you use me?"

While his offer comforts me somewhat, I shake my head. "You know that won't work."

"Yeah, I guess. It's just, it worked once before. I thought maybe..."

I've been over what happened in my room that day hundreds of times, and I still can't explain why I needed to feed from Jack. I haven't had the desire since. Werewolf blood still appeals to my vampire side, but it's a totally visceral reaction. I don't hunger for it. It's kind of like the crappy off-brand cookies one of my supervisors at the call center used to bring in to boost morale—no one really *wanted* those cookies, but because they were there, most of us ate a handful. "I can't explain why it worked. But that's not really surprising, since I can't explain any of this."

The corners of Jack's mouth quirk up in a smile. "It's pretty new to me, too." He brings his hand to my face and strokes my cheek with his thumb. The gesture is all I need to know that he's not repulsed by my need. He understands.

A scent tickles my nostrils and I straighten. Jack sniffs the air. "It's a deer," he says. "That might work—I've met vampires before who lived entirely off animal blood. I can help you catch it if you want. I can flank it and drive it toward you."

Animal blood. Why didn't I think of that before? In my mind, the only options have been werewolf blood—which won't help me—or human blood. If I can take what I need from animals, people wouldn't need to factor into the equation at all. "Okay."

Jack shifts and runs off. No sooner is he out of sight than my palms begin to sweat and blood rushes in my ears. The hunger in my stomach is so sharp now that it's making my vision blur. I can't wait this long between feedings again. My mind is foggy, and I have little doubt that if I were near people, I wouldn't be able to control myself.

Crashes sound in the woods about ten yards ahead of me. I force myself to focus and prepare to run. The deer appears through the brush ahead of me, and I sprint after it. Even in human form, my speed is well beyond that of any normal person. When the doe catches sight of me, she changes direction, but she can't get away from me fast enough. I leap, landing on her back and knocking her to the forest floor. My teeth burn as they lengthen, and I sink them into her soft neck. It must be some kind of vampire instinct, because I know exactly where to bite. The fur tickles my face, but I ignore it. I expect the animal to thrash, but instead she seems to calm as I drink. I wonder if there's something in my bite making her docile.

It doesn't taste as good as what Luke gave me at the mansion, and it's different from when I drank from Jack, but it still satisfies me. When I've had enough to quench the hunger, I pull away and climb off the doe's back. After spitting out some fur, I check to make sure she's all right. A twig snaps behind me and I smell campfire. "Do you think she'll be okay?"

Jack circles the doe, whose eyes are heavy. He strokes her head and peers at her. "I think so. She looks like she wants to take a snooze."

"She didn't fight. I expected her to fight."

He nods like this doesn't exactly surprise him. "I think vampire venom may have a mild paralytic in it."

I pat the deer on the back and murmur a "thank you" before turning and heading toward the enclave. It's strange how the place seems to pull me to it. I wait until Jack is at my side before speaking. "Venom?"

He nods. "I'm not sure entirely how it works, but I know vampires have venom. Maybe a couple kinds. A bite to feed won't necessarily turn a human into a vampire. I think whatever venom they use for that needs to be specifically injected for that purpose."

"So it's different with wolves?"

"Yes. The way a person is turned into a werewolf works more like a virus than a venom. There are some immortals who dedicate their lives to figuring this stuff out. I only know a bit that I've picked up over the years."

I can't help smiling. "I guess with as many years as you've got under your belt, you can't help having picked up some things."

He looks at me out of the corner of his eye. "Are you trying to say I'm old?"

I hold my hands up innocently. "You look fabulous for over a hundred."

Jack laughs and reaches for my hand, and we

walk at a leisurely pace through the woods. I inhale deeply, allowing myself to relax on the exhale. For a few minutes, I push all the complications from my mind and pretend the two of us are just a normal couple out for a relaxing stroll. But as we near the enclave, Jack's easy-going posture tightens and the smile slips from his face. I hear his voice in my head: *Mel, Dakota, and Sawyer, meet me at my house.* The words drip with a kind of authority I can't put into words. Even though the command wasn't aimed at me, I feel the weight of it.

"Someone told that witch about you being my half. We need to find out who."

He shifts and takes off at a run toward his house. I do the same. I want to know who betrayed us just as badly as he does—perhaps more.

By the time we arrive, Jack's front door is open, and Dakota, Mel, and Sawyer are standing inside. Sawyer wears a white tank top and a pair of sweatpants. His hair is damp with perspiration. He was probably down at the gym when he got the call. Mel's appearance couldn't be more different. She stands with her shoulders back, her long dark hair pulled into a low ponytail at the base of her neck. Her face is impassive. Dakota's expression is mildly baffled.

"I'm assuming the meeting didn't go as well as we'd hoped," Sawyer says as Jack and I shift back into human form.

"You could say that," Jack says, his voice cold.

Mel crosses her arms over her chest. "What's this—"

Jack silences her with a look. "A witch on the council knew that Ava was my half. Who told her?"

His words aren't a command. Jack wants the guilty party to come forward willingly. I look from Mel to Sawyer to Dakota and back again. While Sawyer's and Dakota's eyebrows have hiked upward, Mel's expression hasn't changed.

Seconds tick by before Mel finally speaks. "Maybe it was that witch friend of yours. Cassandra, is it?"

Jack shakes his head before she's even finished speaking. "I was there. She was just as shocked as we were. Cassandra would never betray me."

He says it with such certainty. I don't doubt it's true, but I can't help wondering why he's so convinced. What kind of history do the two of them have?

Mel shrugs. "Well, maybe it was Skye then."

Jack steps in close to her, snarling. "Are you really going to try to hide behind the dead?"

Mel doesn't shrink away. "If you have something to say, say it."

"I know it was you," Jack says, his voice low and dangerous. "I didn't command secrecy when I told the three of you about Ava being my half because I believed I could trust you. And you probably would've kept my secret if Ava hadn't bested you and taken your place in the pack."

Mel's lips draw back, revealing her teeth. "This halfbreed isn't fit even to be a member of our pack. She's the reason Skye is dead, but you can't see that. You're too smitten to see her for what she really is."

Movement outside the still-open front door catches my attention. The rest of the pack is assembling at the base of the hill. "Jack, did you call them?"

"No," Mel says, stalking toward the door. "I did."

My stomach sinks. No good can come of this. Jack, Sawyer, Dakota, and I follow as Mel addresses the pack. "Our alpha is putting us in danger by allowing this hybrid to live among us. It's only a matter of time before more packs come for her. How many more of us will die protecting her? How many more will Jack sacrifice to save his *half*?"

A rumble of murmurs spreads through the crowd. I'm stabbed by this new betrayal. She has no right to be the one to tell the pack about Jack and me, yet here she is, announcing it to everyone.

"Stand down, Mel," Jack growls, striding toward her. "You are no longer fit to be a leader of this pack."

She tips her head back and laughs. "That's rich, coming from you. You're no longer fit to be our alpha."

Beside me, Sawyer inhales sharply. "Think about what you're saying," he murmurs, a hint of warning in his voice.

Her eyes flick to him for a moment. "I know what I'm saying." She turns her attention back to the wolves. "Jack no longer has the best interests of this pack at heart. I demand Jack leave this pack at once—or face the consequences."

Another murmur ripples through the group, and all eyes turn to Jack. He squares his shoulders. "I will not leave this pack."

The two of them start down the hill to where those assembled are already forming a large circle. Sawyer begins walking toward them and I follow, keeping pace with him. "What's going on?"

"What does it look like?" he asks, his voice barely above a whisper. "If an alpha or a beta believes a member is a danger to the pack or to pack unity, they can cast them out. The exception is the alpha. Any pack member can call an alpha's loyalty into question. But you can't just cast out an alpha—he has to be beaten. They're going to fight, and whoever wins gets to stay."

Icy dread trickles into the pit of my stomach. "What happens to the loser?"

Sawyer keeps his eyes trained ahead of him. "It's a fight to the death."

CHAPTER SEVENTEEN

HIS WORDS freeze me in place. I must've heard wrong. But the pack is arranging itself in a large circle, the same way it did both times I fought Mel. Except those times, the consequence of losing wasn't so dire. "A fight to the death?" I demand, chasing after Sawyer. "You can't let them do that."

He stops and rounds on me. "I can't stop them. The challenge was issued and accepted. Unless someone forfeits, one of them has to die." Without giving me a chance to absorb this information, Sawyer continues down the hill.

I inhale deeply, trying to will myself to relax. I like the idea of forfeit being an option. Maybe no one will have to die today. I jog down the hill and join the circle.

Dakota walks into the center of the ring. Her

shoulders are drawn back and her chin is raised, but an air of unease surrounds her. I doubt she imagined having to deal with something like this on her first day as alpha female. "Mel has challenged Jack's place in this pack. As you know, if neither party forfeits, one must die. As Jack is the one who has been challenged, he gets to choose which form they fight in."

Lillie squeezes in beside me. There's sadness in her eyes. As Jack announces he elects to fight in wolf form, my heartbeat begins to thunder in my ears. I was just getting used to the idea of Jack as my half—of him being in my life as a boyfriend, or something more. I don't know if I can handle watching him kill someone right in front of me. "This won't be so bad, right?" I murmur to Lillie, hoping she can help calm me down. "When Mel realizes she can't win, she'll forfeit and everything will be okay."

She shifts uncomfortably. "It's not that easy. Even if Mel wants to forfeit, she can't stay in the pack after something like this. She'll have to be strong enough to pull herself away from the pack bonds. If she can't, Jack still has to kill her. He can't have a disloyal wolf among us."

I gulp. That wasn't at all what I wanted to hear.

Dakota rejoins the rest of the pack as Mel and Jack walk toward the center of the circle. They shift,

Jack moving just a split second faster. I'm more than a little relieved he's chosen to change forms for the fight. I wouldn't want Mel to pull some kind of dirty trick like she did on me with that silver knife.

As Mel darts forward, trying to get in an early hit, Lillie slips her hand into mine and squeezes it.

Jack twists to avoid Mel's opening salvo, but he's not fast enough to get in a hit. The two circle each other for several moments before Jack attempts his own offensive. A sharp yelp is enough for me to know he's managed a bite on Mel's back, but she doesn't stop fighting. Once she shakes him off, she goes in for a swipe.

I don't want to watch, but I can't turn away. For each move one of them makes, the other responds in kind. The two are evenly matched. I don't know how long the fight will go on. Are there time limits on a challenge of this magnitude? Or could they be at this for hours? Jack is probably already tired from the run from the council meeting. What if he can't keep up with Mel? For the first time, I wonder if there's a possibility that Jack won't come out the winner.

No. I won't let that happen. I don't know what I can do to stop it, but there's no way I'm letting Mel kill Jack.

Mel backs up a few paces, and I wonder whether she's considering giving up. But no sooner has the thought formed than Mel darts forward, catching Jack off guard and knocking him to the ground. Lillie's grip on my hand tightens as I suck in a breath. Mel is on top of Jack, and despite the way he twists his body, he's not able to get out from under her. I want to go to him, to knock her off and make sure he's safe, but Lillie's grip on my hand roots me to my spot.

Mel bears her teeth, but before she can go in for the kill, Jack rocks in such a way that he knocks her off balance. He draws his lips back, but I look away before he can clamp his mouth around Mel's neck.

"Forfeit!" cries a choked voice. The sound surprises me so much that I turn back to see Mel shifting slowly back into human form. "I forfeit!"

Jack releases his grip on her neck and backs away before shifting back to human himself. He looms over her, staring at her as if looking at a stranger. "Can you leave this pack?"

I expect her to answer, so when pain tears through my body, I'm taken so off guard I nearly double over. It's as if someone has taken a knife to part of me and is carving it away.

In her spot on the ground, Mel pants and sweat beads on her forehead. Lillie squeezes my fingers and covers her mouth with her free hand. I think I understand what's happening: Everyone in the pack can feel Mel's attempt to separate. The pain is blinding—worse than anything I've ever experienced, and that includes the night I was stabbed by the mugger. Does it feel like this for her, too?

A scream tears itself from Mel's throat, and the stinging in my body ebbs. She's done it. She's pulled free from our pack bonds.

Jack lifts his chin. "Mel is cast out. As of this moment, she is a lone wolf, forbidden from ever stepping foot or paw on this territory again."

With obvious effort, Mel drags herself to her feet. At the far side of the circle, pack members begin to separate, creating a hole through which she can pass. "He doesn't care about any of you—not since he found his halfbreed half," she calls as she staggers forward. "He won't protect you if it means losing her."

Jack steps forward into the sunlight, and I detect some of the injuries he sustained during the fight through the rips in his shirt. Even though the blood still glistens, the wounds are already knitting themselves back together. "I will release anyone who wants to go with her," Jack says, his voice ringing clear through the air.

For several moments, no one moves. All the members of the pack are abnormally still. It's not until Mel reaches a spot outside the circle and turns to face the rest of us that some begin to shuffle.

There are a dozen in all. I've spoken with each of them in passing. Some—like a tall, burly man named Tanner—don't surprise me. He's regarded me with increasing trepidation since Mel failed to reclaim the spot I took from her. But the two women who step cautiously toward Mel send ripples of betrayal through my system. Fiona and Marisol are both submissive wolves who have been nothing but kind and welcoming to me since my arrival. Have they been lying the whole time? Or did their opinion of me change when they realized what I am?

More shocks of pain jolt through my system, but nothing as terrible as what happened when Mel separated herself. I think I understand why this is different: Jack is allowing these wolves to leave freely. Still, the pain of their separation slices through my soul.

As the defectors reach Mel, they all shift and take off into the woods. Once the thudding of their paws dissipates, Jack reaches his hand toward me, inviting me to join him. When I'm at his side, he addresses the remaining members of the pack. "Some of what Mel said is true: Ava is a hybrid, which you already knew. She's also my half. I didn't share this with the entire pack because I wanted to give her the chance to adjust. I wanted to allow her to choose when to tell you all. And I will do anything to keep her safe." He laces his fingers through mine. "But what Mel failed to realize is that promise extends to all of you. I'm still the same alpha you've known—some of you for decades. I will not willfully put any of you in undue danger. But you deserve to know that danger is coming. There are those who want to harm Ava, and we will protect her—not because she's special or better, and not because she's my half, but because she's a member of this pack, and we take care of our own."

Cheers of ascent shoot up around the circle, and even though I force a smile, my stomach twists. I don't want anyone else put in danger because of me. We just lost thirteen members of our pack—wolves who have been with Jack longer than I've been changed, wolves who chose to abandon their family because they don't trust him anymore. No, it's not him they don't trust—it's me. As much as I'd like to believe that those who remain are loyal and believe in me, I can't shake a nagging feeling in the back of my mind.

In the weeks since I was turned, our pack is down fourteen members. How many more will we lose before all is said and done?

CHAPTER EIGHTEEN

I LIE on my back across Lillie's bed, my eyes fixed on the ceiling. I don't know if she's even noticed I'm not paying attention anymore.

It's been two days since Mel left the pack. Two days since Cassandra wasn't able to escape from the witches whose council she used to lead. I want to be doing something—anything—to be helpful. Instead I'm slowly losing my mind.

"I'm not sure if I should go for a pure white on the baseboard or something more like an eggshell," Lillie says. She's had me looking at color swatches for the last hour. I feel the last of my sanity slipping away. Yes, I can recognize that there are subtle differences between the colors she's suggesting, but they don't seem significant enough to warrant this kind of discussion. It seems every time I state an opinion, she goes out of her way to disagree—even when my opinion agrees with her initial stance.

My stomach growls and inspiration strikes. I prop myself on my elbow. “Let’s go grab something to eat. I bet there are leftovers in the cooler at the meeting house we could snag.”

Despite the fact that I have a fully functioning kitchen in the house, there’s virtually no food in the refrigerator. With everything that’s happened since I came to live here, I haven’t exactly had a chance to run to the grocery store. All that’s here now is what Lillie brought over from her old house, and those supplies are rapidly dwindling.

She bites her lower lip. “I’d feel much better taking a break if I knew I had my colors nailed down.”

I roll my eyes and stand. “If I have to stare at these color swatches anymore, I’m going to gouge out my eyes. I might have some clarity after I get some food in me.” I head out the door, and she’s at my side in an instant.

“We should go to a restaurant in town. After that, we could go to the grocery store. You know what they say—don’t go to the grocery store on an empty stomach or you’ll end up buying stuff you don’t need.”

I press my lips together, considering the options. I haven’t been around humans since I transitioned. While I still have deer blood in my system from the other day, I'm not sure I'm ready to risk being in public yet. I'd feel much better going if I knew I'd be outnumbered. Lillie is strong, but I don't know if she would stand a chance against me if I go full-on blood hungry.

"I don't think there's anything in the cooler right now, anyway," she continues. "I heard some of the guys talking about raiding it for snacks to eat while they watch the Tigers game."

I pause and turn to look at her. She's acting strange. "Why don't you want me to go to the meeting house?"

She shakes her head, but an expression flickers across her face that she's not quick enough to hide. "It's not that—I just don't want you to waste a trip."

I raise my eyebrows. "You're lying to me."

"No, I'm not," she says, but panic flashes in her eyes.

Any lingering doubt I may have had evaporates. There's something going on at the meeting house and Lillie doesn't want me there. Ignoring her further protests, I open the front door and shift before setting off at a run toward the hill at the center of the enclave. Although I'm fast in human form, it's no match for the speed of my wolf. About a minute later, I reach the meeting house and shift back as I step onto the porch. A glance through the window reveals most of the remaining pack, including Jack, Dakota, Cecily, and Sawyer. The windows are closed, but when I focus, I can hear the words being spoken inside. It takes a minute for me to realize what's they're planning: a mission to rescue Cassandra.

This is why Lillie wanted me to stay at the house. This is why we spent the last hour talking about color combinations instead of going to the gym, and it's why Jack stopped by earlier to insist I take a day off from training.

I stalk to the nearest door and pull it open. An uneasy silence falls over the crowd as their eyes land on me. I look at Jack. "Is there a reason I wasn't invited to this meeting?"

After a quick glance at Sawyer, Jack stands from the metal folding chair and crosses to me, smiling all the way. He reaches forward and strokes his hand against my cheek. "We'll talk about this later, okay? Lillie said she needed you today, so—"

If he thinks a little bit of charm is enough to make me forget how angry I am, he's wrong. Even though the way he's looking at me melts my insides and sparks skip across my skin where he touches my face, I refuse to be put off. "You put her up to it, didn't you? You made her fabricate a reason to keep me in the house."

The pack members shift in their seats and a

muscle in Jack's jaw jumps. "Now's not the time for an argument," he says, his voice low. "It's bad for pack unity to see a high-ranking wolf, such as yourself, fighting with the alpha."

"I'm not fighting with my *alpha*, I'm fighting with my *half*," I grumble, crossing my arms over my chest. Still, I'm not blind enough not to see his point, so I turn to the others in the room. "Would you all step outside for a minute?"

Two dozen sets of eyes flick from me to Jack. After a beat, he nods. "Do what she says."

I wait until everyone filters outside. "Why don't you want me here?"

He sighs. "I asked Lillie to keep you at the house today because we're discussing a plan to get Cassandra back from the witches, and—"

"I want to come," I say, not letting him finish.

He closes his eyes for a moment before continuing. "And I knew you'd want to come. Ava, don't you get how dangerous it would be? Kiara and the other witches on the council made it pretty clear they see you as a threat to the balance of nature. They don't think you should be allowed to exist."

I understand what he's telling me—I was there, after all—but I shake my head. "I'm not staying behind. I want to help."

He settles his hands on my shoulders. "I need you to help by staying behind to watch over the territory."

"Sawyer can do that. Or Dakota. Or Cecily. Or—who's the fourth female now?"

Jack growls.

"I don't care what you say—I'm going to help you save Cassandra."

He stares at me for a beat before sliding his hands down my arms and leaning his head down until he touches my forehead with his. "Okay. If you really want to come that badly, I won't stand in your way."

Before I can respond, the back door swings open and heavy footfalls sound as the rest of the pack comes back into the meeting house. "How'd they know we were done talking?"

Jack shrugs. "It's been a minute. Sometimes commands can be interpreted pretty literally."

I can't help smiling. "I bet it's crossed your mind to use an alpha command on me."

The corners of his mouth twitch. "Maybe."

JACK'S GRAY WOLF leads the pack forward. The sunlight slants through the trees at a steep angle. The sun will set soon.

He comes to a stop and we all freeze in place. An instant later, he shifts back to human form and pulls a necklace out from beneath his shirt to consult it. He explained to me before we left that he's worn this talisman for decades. Cassandra gave it to him before the time of telephones when the two of them still moved around a lot, so he could always find her, no matter what. I wanted to ask just how long they've known each other and what kind of relationship they've had over the years, but it wasn't the time.

Jack points and I hear his voice in my head. *There's a cabin up ahead. Cassandra must be in there. First wave, get ready.*

While Jack finally relented and allowed me to accompany them on this mission, I had to promise I'd stay hidden from any witches who might be around. I understand it's for the best, but it hurts knowing I can't do anything to help. Cassandra is only in this situation because she wanted to stand up for me. I owe it to her to rescue her from her imprisonment.

Jack and six other wolves move forward. In the back of my mind, I'm aware of what's going on through the link I share with the others in the pack. He told me it's something we could experience in human form too, but it takes more effort to locate it, because the human mind is so much more complex. But now, as a wolf on the hunt, part of my mind is constantly aware of the pack members surrounding me. Even though I'm too far back to see, I know there's movement in the window. I feel the sharp sense of betrayal when Jack recognizes Stephen, one of the witches from the council. The scent on the air is enough to confirm there are only two people in the building. With that knowledge, Jack nods, and the first wave descends on the cabin.

My muscles tense as I wait. It feels like an eternity before I hear glass shattering. The plan is for the first group to break into the house and distract Cassandra's captor before the second wave moves in to rescue her. Even though Jack prepared me for it, the howls and stabs of pain that shoot through my system nearly take my breath away. The witches wouldn't leave the cabin unprotected, of course, and there are traps set with magic that have impacted four of the wolves who went in for the first distraction. I can sense from the pack bond that while they were hurt, they will be all right. I sense through my link with Jack when the second wave moves in.

I promised to stay out of sight, but I need to see what's going on with my own eyes. I creep forward on silent paws, careful to keep myself hidden among the bushes. The cabin comes into sight just as Jack shifts back to human form. He's at the front door. He kicks it open, but when he goes to cross the threshold, he can't. It's like there's an invisible barrier keeping him out.

A murmur spreads through the link binding all of us together. *Silver dust.* I'm able to glean from the minds of the others that witches can enhance the dust with magic and use it to form an impenetrable barrier for werewolves. Stephen must have sprinkled it across the threshold and on the windowsills in case any weres came for Cassandra. No matter how hard they try, none of my pack members will be able to get into the house.

Except me.

Jack's voice is in my head, telling me to stay where I am, begging me to give him a minute to figure this out, but I ignore him and emerge from my hiding place. I'm the only one who can save her. Waiting doesn't give us the upper hand—action does. If we stand around, it only gives Stephen more time to cast spells against us. If we retreat, he can hide Cassandra somewhere else. He might even be able to hide her with magic to keep us from finding her again.

I run full out and pass by Jack in an instant. When I leap over the threshold, Stephen's eyes widen. I take advantage of his shock and run to where Cassandra sits tied to a chair. As I bite through the ropes, a familiar scent greets me. Wolfsbane. The bindings have been soaked in it, but it doesn't slow me down.

As I'm tearing through the last rope, a searing pain shoots through my back. I don't have to turn to know what happened: Stephen stabbed me. A howl tears itself from my throat, and I hear Jack's voice yelling, swearing, threatening Stephen with the violence that will befall him once Jack gets his hands on him.

I struggle to get to my paws, but the pain in my back is too severe. I can't support my own weight—but I have to. I have to get to Jack.

Cassandra jumps to her feet and Stephen lunges for her, but she picks up the chair she was tied to and swings it with enough force to knock him backward. I hear the sick crack of his head on a countertop, but I can't turn to assess the damage. I look up at her, willing her to understand I want her to leave, to get somewhere safe, but she doesn't. Instead she crouches down, and with a strength I'm shocked she possesses, picks me up and takes slow, heavy steps toward the door.

As soon as she crosses the threshold onto the porch, she crumples, and the two of us collapse onto the weathered boards of the porch. Jack drops to his knees, diverting his attention between the two of us to check if we're all right.

"I'm fine, Jack," Cassandra murmurs, her voice weak. "Tend to your half."

Jack leans in close to my face. "I'm going to pull

out the stake," he says, his voice even.

I whimper in response, clenching my teeth as he grips the object. A sizzling sound reaches my ears and the scent of burnt flesh overwhelms me, but I don't understand what's happening until Jack drops a silver spike to the porch beside me. There's no protective grip anywhere on the weapon, and Jack pulled it out with his bare hand. Even now, he breathes heavily through his teeth as he studies the damage on his palm.

An engine rumbles, getting closer with each second. A Jeep hurtles through the trees and Jack lifts me in his arms. Another pack member—a white and gray wolf named Angela—shifts to human and lifts Cassandra, following Jack to the car. Jack deposits me in the back seat before thanking the driver and climbing behind the steering wheel. Once Cassandra is safely in the passenger seat, Jack puts the engine in gear and drives away from the house. Through the window, I see the other wolves running back into the forest.

A stinging burn sears through my back, and I know the spot where I was stabbed is already healing. When I feel strong enough, I shift back to human form and check on Cassandra. She's weak. I don't know what the witches did to her, but she's missing much of the vitality I've grown to associate with her presence.

"She'll be okay," Jack murmurs. "She has to be."

While the words comfort me, I get the feeling he's trying to convince himself most of all.

CHAPTER NINETEEN

THERE'S A BED waiting at Maggie's house when we get back to the enclave. No sooner does Jack deposit Cassandra onto the mattress than Maggie shoos him out of the room, insisting she needs to do a preliminary examination before she has any idea what kind of treatment Cassandra might need.

Jack growls, but he allows the submissive wolf to push him out the door.

Lillie enters the house as we step out of the hallway. Her brown eyes widen when they land on me and her hand flies up to cover her mouth. "Oh my gosh—did they torture her?"

My brow knits. "I don't think so. Why?"

She points. "Whose blood is all over you two?"

The front of Jack's shirt is smeared with red, and gory streaks stripe the fabric covering my stomach. I sigh and shake my head. "It's mine. A d-bag he-witch stabbed me in the back with a silver spike."

Just when I thought her eyes couldn't widen any more, they go full-on circular. "Why are you still on your feet?" she demands, crossing to me. "Why isn't anyone checking you out?"

Before I can stop her, Lillie is pulling up my shirt to expose my back. Her thin fingers press gently but firmly against my skin as she examines the area still sticky with blood. "I don't understand—I'm not seeing the wound."

I reach for the hem of my shirt and tug it back down, hoping she gets the hint. "I'm fine."

After a brief struggle, she removes her hands and comes around to face me. "Are you sure it was silver? You haven't been gone that long. If it was really silver, it would still be mending."

Jack holds out his hands, palms up. The flesh is shiny and red—still healing from the scorch marks left by his contact with the spike. "It was silver, all right."

When Lillie turns to me, brow furrowed, I shrug. "Perks of being a hybrid?"

Her jaw drops and she shakes her head in wonder. "I can't believe it. I've never seen a were heal from silver that fast."

I manage to smile, but my amusement is

tempered by the gnawing sensation growing in the pit of my stomach. It's not as bad as the burning I know will come soon, but it's impossible to ignore. I haven't had blood since Jack helped me catch the doe the other night. I'm not sure whether it's simply time for me to feed again or if healing from the injury burned through whatever was left in my system, but one thing is for sure: I'll need more to drink soon.

Lillie disappears down the hall and I assume she's going to check on Cassandra and Maggie. Jack stands still as a statue, staring straight ahead, his eyes slightly unfocused. His expression is dark, haunted. I wish I knew what was going on in his head.

Lillie returns, a woven basket in her hands. She nods toward the couch. "Have a seat, Jack. I want to look at your hands."

For a second he doesn't move. It's not until Lillie opens her mouth to repeat herself that he complies. She perches on the cushion beside him and takes up one of his hands in hers.

She's too close. I don't like the way she's touching him. She's bending down over his palm, her long blonde hair spilling around her face, brushing against his leg. My muscles coil, ready to spring, and my lips curl. I want to pull her away, to teach her never to lay a finger on him again.

I squeeze my eyes shut. What's going on? Lillie is my friend, and she's obviously just tending to Jack's injuries. So why do I want to fight her?

My eyes begin to prickle and I realize what's happening. I'm not upset about what's going on—my wolf is. I sigh, releasing a breathy chuckle.

Jack's attention flickers to me for the first time in minutes. "What's so funny?"

Heat rises in my cheeks and I shake my head, feeling silly. "Nothing. It's just... maybe I should leave until Lillie's finished."

Lillie turns to me, too, and the burning on my face intensifies. "My wolf doesn't like how close the two of you are," I explain.

She leaps backward, putting an entire cushion of space between herself and Jack. "I'm so sorry—I didn't even think..."

I shake my head. "Seriously, don't worry. Take care of him. I'll go. I should probably get changed anyway."

Before either of them has a chance to say anything, I head out of the house. As I follow the curve of the road to my house, I try to make sense of what just happened. If I hadn't caught myself, would I have fought Lillie? All because she was touching Jack?

Half.

The word echoes through my mind, making me

jump. I spin in a circle, scanning the area to make sure no one saw me, but stop short when I realize how silly I must look.

I've never felt jealousy like that before in my life. My wolf doesn't understand the same complexities and subtleties I do, so seeing Lillie close to Jack angered her. Because he's my half.

I've done my best not to think too much about the implications of the two of us sharing parts of the same soul. I can understand intellectually how it's a huge deal—but I struggle with the personal implications. Do I love Jack? And if I do, is it because I want to, or because I have to?

I shake my head as I climb the stairs to my porch. I can't think about it right now—not with the hunger building inside me. I change quickly, throwing the ripped and blood-stained shirt in the garbage and setting the jeans aside to inspect later, before heading back outside.

My eyes sweep the tree line, inspecting it for the best place to begin my trek into the woods. I'm not sure how far I'll have to go before I run into an animal large enough to satisfy my need. Birds and squirrels skitter in the branches, but in addition to the fact that I'm not sure I could catch one, I'm afraid if I did, I'd drink too much and accidentally kill it.

I've just stepped off the porch when Jack

appears from around a curve. He smiles when he sees me, the darkness that haunted his face earlier evaporated—at least for the moment. The fire in my belly is growing by the instant, sending prickles of pain through my chest and into my arms, but I steel myself against it. I can't simply run into the forest now.

Jack's grin grows as we near each other. "On your way back to make sure Lillie isn't using her wiles on me?"

I'm about to defend myself, to remind him how new this whole werewolf thing still is to me, when I catch the teasing glint in his eyes. "You think this is hilarious, don't you?"

He shrugs and I nudge his shoulder playfully. "What can I say? I liked seeing you all possessive. Very sexy." He snakes an arm around my back and pulls me flush against his body. The mischievous sparkle from moments ago is gone, replaced by a smolder that hollows out my stomach, displacing the ravenous fire brimming there. He kisses me, crushing my lips and taking my breath away. My wolf approves and urges me to return his embrace, to press myself closer still, but the fire inside me rekindles. I need to feed.

When I push him away, disappointment flashes in his eyes. "What's wrong?" He glances over both shoulders and the corners of his mouth twitch.

"Would you like to move this inside?"

"No," I say quickly, realizing too late it's the wrong response. I absolutely want to continue what we're doing, and being somewhere alone with Jack has never been more appealing. "I mean, *yes*—just, not right now."

His eyebrows draw together. "I've got to tell you—you're sending some pretty mixed signals."

I sigh. "I'm not trying to. I'm just... I was about to go for a run."

"Sounds great." He takes a step back and turns toward the woods. When I don't imitate his posture, he tilts his head. "Unless you don't want company."

I twist my fingers together, my gaze dropping. "I kind of wanted to go alone. After everything that happened today I'm a little... hungry."

"And you didn't think you could tell me?"

Embarrassment sweeps through me. I'm not sure why it didn't occur to me to tell him to begin with. It's not as if he hasn't helped me hunt already. "I'm sorry. I just feel so weird about it. Like, I'm just going to go off and suck some blood. Be back later."

He brushes his fingers under my chin until I look up at him. "I hate vampires—have longer than I've been a wolf. But you are not one of them. Don't ever feel like you need to hide who you are from me."

I allow his words to sink into me, to calm me.

He's right, of course. There's not one thing he's done since learning I'm a hybrid that would lead me to believe I have to keep anything from him. "Okay. But I do think I want to do this on my own. This time."

"Of course. Whatever you need."

I try to step around him, but he stills my progress long enough to press a kiss to my lips. By the time he releases me, I'm smiling. "Will you be at your place?"

He nods. "Probably there or with Cassandra. Find me when you're done."

Feeling his eyes on me, I shift and run off toward the nearest set of trees. I've done a lot of running in the last few days—mostly toward or away from dangerous situations. But this is nothing like that. I allow myself to feel the ground, to smell the air, to feel the wind as it rushes through my fur. It's exhilarating.

I run as fast as I can, testing the limits of my speed. I'm getting farther and farther from the enclave, but I'm always aware of its location in space. I get the sense that no matter how far away I get, I'll always know exactly where home is.

For a long time, I concern myself more with speed and agility than stealth, and the noise I generate scares off all the wildlife. Eventually I slow down and decide to test my skills at hunting. Last time I had Jack's help, but I can't rely on that all the time. I need to know I can catch prey myself, that if it comes down to it, I can do it on my own.

It takes a long time before I catch the scent. A deer. I don't know how I'm so sure before I can even see it, but I am. I approach it as stealthily as I can. Night has fallen in earnest now, and I see it lying down among some trees. It's not exactly the kind of hunting I need to practice, but I figure for tonight, simply locating it on my own is good enough.

I shift back to human before drawing near to it. I'm able to get within feet before it senses my presence, but before it can get to its hooves, I'm on it. I sink my teeth into its neck and drink long gulps. Like last time, I don't take enough to harm it, but before I climb off its back, a twig snaps and I freeze. The scent on the air tells me someone is approaching. Someone familiar. For a split second I smile, the familiarity in the aroma making me think it's Jack. But it's not him.

In a flash, I'm on my feet and I've spun to face the man who approaches. "Luke?"

The moonlight filtering through the branches makes his blonde hair look silver. He smiles, teeth flashing. "Fancy meeting you here."

"Are you stalking me?" I can't think of any other reason he might be in the forest at this time of night. Unless he's on the hunt himself, but given my interactions with him so far, I highly doubt he's interested in animal blood.

He holds up his hands innocently. "Don't flatter yourself. I was on my way to a favorite spot of mine when I sensed you were near. You're closer to civilization than I think you realized."

The weight of the situation crashes on me. What am I doing so far from the enclave alone? I'm vulnerable out here. I should've let Jack come with me. What if Luke pulls the same trick he did when I showed up at the mansion? What if he convinces me to go with him? Or, worse, what if he's figured out what I am? So many people already want to do me harm—is he one more to add to the list?

The corner of Luke's mouth quirks upward. "You're afraid of me. May ask what's happened? If memory serves, you had quite a different opinion last time I saw you. Are the wolves who spirited you away brainwashing you or something?"

I can't suppress a sneer. "Like you care."

"Normally, I wouldn't. But I won't lie—you fascinate me." He takes a step closer, and I direct all my willpower into not shrinking back. "Our kind don't usually spend time with dogs, and I can smell them on you." I blink, and when I reopen my eyes, he's standing so close his breath tickles my face. He inhales deeply, his nose wrinkling. "Why are they so interested in you, anyway? And why do you want to stay with them?"

Relief sweeps through me. He doesn't know what I am. Good—too many do already. "That's my business."

His face hardens. I can tell he's the kind of person who's used to people giving him what he wants. "I could make you tell me."

After our last encounter, I have no doubt he could. Cassandra told me about how a sire can impose his will on the vampire he created. As much as I want to dare him, I'm afraid he'll follow through on his threat. And if he starts forcing me to talk, what will he learn? What else could he make me do?

He traces a finger down my cheek. "You should leave them and come with me. I'll show you what life can really be like for our kind. You don't have to feed on poor woodland creatures."

I take a step back. "What would you rather I do? Drink the blood of unsuspecting people instead? No thanks."

He tilts his head and studies me. "Have you ever tasted human blood? Besides when you came to me. You burned through that too quickly to really appreciate the taste, the effect."

I swallow, fighting to hold his gaze. I don't want to tell him the truth—besides animal blood and what he gave me, the only other kind I've had is Jack's.

But he doesn't seem to expect me to answer. "You have no idea what you're missing out on. Come with me. I promise, if you don't like what I have to offer, you can go back to your pets."

A voice in the back of my mind urges me to go with him. He could show me more than I could ever imagine. I'm not living up to my full potential, and Luke can teach me so much more than Jack can.

No sooner do I think his name than his face flashes in my mind. Jack. My alpha—my other half. As alluring as Luke's offer is, I don't want to leave Jack. The whole time I've known him, the only thing he's wanted is to take care of me. He could have pressed me to merge before the council meeting, but he refused to take advantage of the situation to force me to do something I'm not ready for. He respects me and my needs. Luke only cares about his own.

But when I look into his electric blue eyes, my resolve wavers again. What if he's right and I really am missing out on something?

I open my mouth, but before I can speak, a sound catches my attention. The scent comes next, and I immediately recognize it for what it is—a vampire.

Luke curses. "I'll be right there," he calls.

I don't wait for him to turn back to me. Taking advantage of his momentary distraction, I run. My human form isn't as agile as my wolf, but I wait until I am far out of Luke's line of sight before shifting.

I want to go back to Jack. I want to go home.

CHAPTER TWENTY

I SMELL THE BONFIRE before I reach the enclave. Joyful shouts rend the air. When I finally emerge through the trees, an orange glow peeks over the top of the meeting house hill. It's not entirely surprising—the pack weres seem to hang out most nights of the week. This week, a party is more important than ever. After Mel's defection and the loss of the dozen who followed her, spending time with those who are left and remembering what being a pack means is crucial.

I should go—but after my interaction with Luke in the woods, I can't bring myself to. Not yet. Maybe after a little time alone or after a really, really hot shower, I'll be in a more social mood. But seeing the man responsible for my vampire side reminds me that our need for pack unity is my fault. If I weren't a hybrid, Mel wouldn't have had the same ammunition against me and Jack. Those who left with her wouldn't have felt their alpha had placed more value on my life than theirs.

Skye would still be alive.

As I follow the curve of the road toward my house, I hope Lillie is still at Maggie's place, keeping watch over Cassandra. If she's at the house, it'll be because she's looking for me, and I doubt anything I could say would make her give up on dragging me to the party.

I release a relieved sigh when the darkened windows of my cabin come into view, but before I can start for it, my eyes are drawn to Jack's. Light spills through the large window at the front of the house, and a flicker tells me Jack is inside.

Suddenly being home alone doesn't sound as appealing. He did want me to come find him when I was done, and the idea of being in his presence calms me. I take off at a run and pad effortlessly up the hill. I don't shift to human until I'm on the porch, and before I can knock, the door swings open.

Jack smiles, holding a wine glass brimming with amber liquid in his outstretched hand. "I was hoping you'd come here instead of checking out the bonfire."

I relieve him of the glass as I step over the

threshold. "You knew I was coming?"

He nods, sweeping his hand toward the black leather couch. "It works better when distances are smaller, but I can sense members of the pack. It's kind of like... feeling their energy." As I settle on the cushions, he crosses to the long counter separating the living room from the kitchen and picks up another full glass of wine. "I knew when you were getting closer to the enclave."

When he settles beside me on the couch, he takes a long sip of wine. I realize I haven't had any and take a tentative taste, not entirely sure what to expect. I've done my share of drinking in my nineteen years, but I've never had occasion to try wine. It's not exactly the drink of choice at the kinds of bars that don't card. I'm surprised by its crispness and the strong fruity undertones.

"This is really good." I feel silly—childish, even—for saying it, but Jack only smiles.

"I'm glad you like it. It's one of my favorites."

My eyebrows hike upward. "You strike me more as a beer guy."

He shrugs. "I do enjoy a good beer, but my father was French. I started drinking wine with dinner as soon as he was sure I wasn't going to spill any."

I sit a little straighter at the mention of his father. On my first night, Lillie mentioned how little she knows about Jack's history, so the casual comment is unexpected. "You haven't told me much about your family."

"There's not much to tell," he says, setting the glass down on the low table in front of us. I recognize his tone immediately—it's the same one I've used a hundred times before when someone would ask me to talk about my past. He doesn't want to talk about his family because something about them still causes him pain after all these years. I'm sure of it.

I take another sip of wine, trying to come up with another topic. "Why aren't you at the bonfire? It seems like something you should attend."

"I put in an appearance already." Some of the tension in his shoulders drains and he picks up his glass again. "Dakota and the betas are there. The two of us could go back later, if you want, but it's not like we need to chaperone things."

Jack draws one leg up onto the couch as he angles himself toward me, his knee brushing against my thigh for a split second. Sparks dance on my skin where he made contact and part of me wonders whether we're the ones in need of a chaperone. My body tingles when I remember how he looked at me before I went for my run—the way he kissed me. I'd needed to stop him then, to quench my hunger, but now there's nothing else vying for my attention. I could get caught up in this moment—in the wine, and the way I always feel around Jack. The wolf within me likes the idea. She senses our connection, and it's all she needs to want to pick up where we left off earlier.

But I am not my wolf, and when Jack leans forward, I bring the wine to my lips and drink until the glass is empty. My distraction gone, I spring to my feet and cross to the counter where the open bottle sits. Jack's eyes are on me as I pour another glass. I take my time at the task and sip a small measure before turning, but he's still watching me.

"What's going on?" he asks.

"Nothing," I say quickly. "Just... wanted more wine." I hold up the glass as evidence.

"You're acting strange." His expression is curious, but not accusatory. "I'm not... making you nervous, am I?"

"No." I sip some more wine. I should slow down, since I'm not sure how the alcohol in it will affect me, but drinking it is an easy stall. My human side and my wolf side are warring within me—one cautious, the other impulsive. I'm not entirely sure how to put everything into words without hurting Jack's feelings.

I set the glass on the counter and return to the couch. I came here tonight because I wanted to see Jack—and he clearly hoped I'd come. The least I can do is attempt to explain what's spinning through my head. "I like being near you. I like the way it feels—the way you make me feel. I'm drawn to you in a way I've never experienced before."

He nods enthusiastically. "It's the same for me. It has to be because we're halves."

He brushes his fingers along the back of my hand and the sensation makes me close my eyes for a moment. There's more I need to say, but it's hard to think straight when he's so near. "But it doesn't change the fact I don't know you very well. You're a hundred-year-old half-French werewolf. Beyond that, you're pretty much a mystery to me."

The corners of his mouth twitch. He exhales through his nose and leans forward to pick up his wine glass, but he doesn't drink from it. Instead he holds it by the stem with his right hand, rests his left elbow on his thigh, and cradles his face in his hand. He spins the glass between his index finger and thumb. "I don't like talking about the past. I got the feeling we were the same in that way."

I take the glass from him and set it down before taking his hand in mine. "Don't tell me about the past. Tell me about you. What are some of your favorite things? What kind of music do you listen to? What's the best thing about being a wolf?" He laces his fingers through mine and I smile. "I want to get to know you so all these romantic feelings don't feel so out of nowhere."

The corner of his mouth quirks upward. "Romantic feelings?"

I tug on his hand. "You know what I mean."

He allows the momentum to pull him inches from my face. "I think I do."

I want to kiss him—badly. If my wolf had it her way, he'd be in my arms already. But I'm not ready to give in. Not yet. Not entirely. I plant a chaste peck on his lips and lean back. He takes the hint and backs up, leaving our hands linked.

"Favorite things?" he asks. "That was the first topic, right?"

We talk for hours. It's incredible how much we can say about ourselves without drawing too deeply on our pasts. The topic does come up, of course. I tell him how my mom died after I was born and how my dad never remarried. I explain how he died of cancer, but I don't dwell on the time I spent bouncing from house to house after that. He mentions his mother was a Cherokee Indian, and that unlike me, he wasn't an only child. But that's all he says about his family. I suppose I can't blame him; it's difficult speaking of the dead. I can't imagine it gets much easier as time passes.

Given he's acquired so much more life experience than I have, I'm surprised how easy it is to talk with him. So much of our time together has consisted of toe-curling kisses and adrenaline-fueled escapes, part of me worried that when it came down to it, we wouldn't have much in common. But conversation flows more freely between the two of us than it does even between Lillie and me—something I was beginning to think was impossible, given that she's quickly become the closest friend I've ever had.

I also learn he's musically inclined. He's spent decades studying and practicing playing piano, guitar, and drums, and he offers to play a few songs for me. His singing voice isn't that of a rock star, but it's warm and clear. I'm pretty sure I could happily listen to it for hours.

I lay my head on the couch's arm rest while he strums the guitar, allowing the music to infuse every part of my being. As the sounds float around me, my body relaxes and I slip into the space between wakefulness and dreams. Jack's songs are like lullabies.

When the music ceases, my eyelids flutter. The gentle weight of a blanket settles over me. "Shh, go back to sleep," Jack murmurs.

I reach for his hand but only manage to find his forearm. "Where you goin'?"

"To bed. It's late."

A measure of my sleepiness evaporates. I don't like the idea of him leaving me. "Can you stay with me?"

His lips curve in a smile. "You're hogging the couch. I won't fit."

I do my best to scoot toward the edge of the cushions, but he's right—there isn't much room. Before I can come up with another solution, Jack bends down and scoops me up in his arms. He lifts me effortlessly and carries me down the hall. The layout of his house isn't dissimilar to mine, and I don't have to open my eyes to know he's taking me toward the bedrooms.

He settles me gently onto a bed and pulls the comforter over me. Moments later, I feel his weight settle on the mattress behind me. He stretches out and snuggles in close, resting his arm across my waist. I sink back against him, my chest rising and falling in time with his. I fit perfectly against his body.

His breath tickles my ear. "Goodnight."

CHAPTER TWENTY-ONE

WHEN I AWAKE the next morning, warm and comfortable, light is spilling in through the window. Odd—I usually pull the shades before I go to sleep.

It's enough to shake away whatever remnants of sleep remain. At once, last night comes flooding back to me: the good—talking with Jack, getting to know him, falling asleep in his arms; and the bad—running into Luke while I went to feed.

I should've told Jack last night. Even though Luke didn't seem to know what I am, and didn't seem to have any particular interest in me beyond curiosity, Jack should know about our run-in. But part of me doesn't want to give him any excuse to track Luke down and snap his neck again. The two have a history—that much is obvious. I don't want to be the reason for any new bad blood.

I roll over and prop myself up on my elbow. Jack is flat on his back, still asleep, his mouth slightly ajar. His brown curls are wild and unruly like they were the first time I saw him. A smile tugs at my lips. He looks so young like this. All the lines of his face are smooth and he looks less like a pack alpha and more like a boy. The thought brings to mind one question I didn't ask last night.

As if he can feel my gaze, Jack twitches, his eyelids fluttering. After a moment, he opens his eyes, smiling when he sees me. "Hey."

On impulse, I lean down and kiss him. "Good morning."

His grin spreads. "Best I've had in a long time." He reaches forward and tucks some hair behind my ear.

I trace my finger along the curve of his cheek. "How old were you when you were changed?" The question spills out of my mouth before I consciously decide to ask it.

The tranquility of the previous moment evaporates as Jack's jaw clenches. A shadow passes over his expression, but it disappears when he exhales. "Twenty-one. I was tracking a vampire, alone—like an idiot. I'd had a run of successes against some leeches leading up to it, and I got it in my head that I was some kind of badass." The corners of his mouth tug upward in a rueful smile.

"Turns out what I thought was one vampire was actually a trio, and they set a trap for me. I fought hard, but I was no match for them. They were about to finish me, but before they could, they took off. A pack of weres was out for a run nearby. A couple of them caught the vampires' scent and came to investigate. One of them found me."

My mind spins with this new information. Jack told me he hated vampires before he became a werewolf, but I didn't know he hunted them. What made him do that? I can't bring myself to ask. He already gave me more detail than was necessary to answer my question; if he wanted me to know more, he'd volunteer specifics. I know he doesn't like to talk about the past, and I'm thankful he decided to share this much with me.

He rolls over and swings his legs over the edge of the bed, and I'm worried I've somehow angered him. But when he stands and turns back to me, his eyes find mine. "We should go check on Cassandra."

He wants me to accompany him. Maybe I didn't push him too far after all.

We agree to meet at the bottom of the hill in fifteen minutes—enough time for a quick shower and a change of clothes. I'm cautious when I enter my house, half expecting Lillie to be sitting on the couch with a mug of tea and a raised eyebrow, but she's not home. I'm not sure whether or not I'm disappointed by her absence. Although in one sense nothing happened between Jack and me last night, in another, so much occurred. I finally feel like there's more between us than instinctual attraction. After sharing who we are with each other, our connection is deeper and fuller than it was before.

After showering, I tie my hair back into a bun and pull on jeans and a tank top. I open the front door just as Jack makes it to the bottom of the hill. I jog to his side and he takes my hand as we start down the road.

The atmosphere at Maggie's house is tense.

"I'm not sure what's wrong with her," Maggie says, her tone hushed. "I figured some rest would do her good, but I don't think she managed to sleep much. She was awake every time I went in to check on her, and as soon as the sun came up, she gave Lillie a list of herbs to go get."

"I want to see her," Jack says.

Maggie shifts her weight from foot to foot. "I don't know if that's the best idea."

Jack levels his gaze on her and she drops her eyes immediately. "Please don't stay long."

She shuffles into the kitchen as Jack and I make our way toward the room where Cassandra is staying. "Maybe you should trust Maggie on this one," I say, careful to keep my voice low.

A muscle in his jaw jumps. "I'll only be a

minute. I just... I need to see her."

Jack twists the doorknob and steps into the room. I follow, doing my best to tamp down the swell of jealousy rising within me. The feeling is ridiculous. Jack has known Cassandra for longer than I've been alive. I don't know their history, but I don't need to. She's a good woman who has done nothing but try to protect me. Yet I still can't shake the tiny stab of betrayal at the idea that Jack may care for her the same way he cares for me. But that's crazy—I'm his half. I'm not in competition with Cassandra in any way.

All my foolish thoughts of jealousy are silenced as soon as I catch a glimpse of Cassandra lying in the middle of the bed. She looks worse than she did on the car ride home yesterday. I'd hoped that after a night in Maggie's care, some of her natural energy would return, but that's not the case. The lines of Jack's jaw harden. He's trying not to let his reaction show, but I can tell Cassandra's appearance is having an effect on him.

He settles down on the chair beside her bed and takes one of her hands gently in both of his. "How are you?"

The corners of her mouth twitch, but she doesn't manage a smile. "I think you know."

Jack releases a heavy breath. "Don't worry. Lillie will be back soon with whatever witchy supplies you sent her for. You can give her painstaking instructions on how to make whatever tea or poultice you need and you'll be on your feet in no time."

She pats the top of his hand with her free one. "Let's hope."

"What did they do to you?" I ask from my spot at the foot of the bed.

"That's the question, isn't it?" Her voice is quiet, thoughtful. "After the two of you escaped, I was knocked out. When I woke up, I was in the cabin where you found me, and I couldn't use magic. I assume the council cast a spell to keep me from being able to—it's what I would've done. But I'm not carrying any talisman, and I had the girls check me over for runes or any other markings, and there were none. I can't think of what they could have done that would still be keeping me from accessing my abilities."

"So you can't do magic at all?" Jack asks.

"I haven't tried," she admits. "I can feel it inside me. I couldn't when I was locked in the cabin. But I don't feel strong enough for spellwork."

Jack offers a tight-lipped smile. "Then I should leave you to rest."

"Tell your nurse wolves they need to rest, too," she says. "I don't think Maggie slept a wink last—"

Jack holds up a hand, silencing her. The hair on

the back of my neck prickles. I sense it, too. There's an intrusion on our territory. Except this time, it's not wolves.

"Vampires," I murmur.

Jack jumps to his feet and strides out the room. "Maggie!"

She pokes her head around the corner, a bewildered expression on her face. "Yes?"

"I need you to shift and stay here to protect Cassandra. Call for some others to come for backup."

Maggie still looks confused, but she nods and does as directed. She probably hasn't detected the invasion yet, but she doesn't hesitate to follow Jack's command.

As he continues toward the front door, I pause, unsure where I should be. But when he crosses the threshold without giving an order for me to stay behind, I jog after him.

"What could the leeches possibly be doing here?" he mutters, scanning the vicinity. Others seem to be aware of the intrusion as well, and I see pack members emerging from indoors before shifting and running off into the woods. "Yes, I invaded their space when I came to rescue you, but retaliation isn't really their thing. They're not a pack the way we are. Their relationships with each other aren't as strong. Besides, if they'd wanted to get back at me for that, they would've done it already. No one else has mentioned run-ins with vampires."

My stomach jolts. I didn't tell him about my encounter with Luke because I didn't want to give him any reason to go looking for a fight. I never considered the interaction could lead to something like this. "Jack?"

He starts slightly as he turns to me, as if he's only just realized I'm still following him. "You should probably stay back and protect Cassandra."

I shake my head. "I have to tell you something."

"It can wait." He takes a step away, but I catch his arm and tug him back.

"No, it can't."

He sighs. "I know what you're going to say. You're going to tell me I can't order you to stay behind every time something dangerous happens. And you're right—you shouldn't have to hide. But you should be smart. The last time someone crossed into our territory, it was about you. Even if it's not the same reason this time, I don't like the idea of having you so close to the vampires in case they figure out something's different about you."

Guilt surges inside me at his words. What if Luke figured out what I am last night when we spoke? I open my mouth to tell him everything, but before I can, he kisses me, crushing my mouth. He shifts and runs into the woods after a few other pack members so quickly I don't get a chance to tell him he's wrong.

My wolf surges within me. I need to get back to protect the vulnerable. I shift before running toward Maggie's house. There are already five others joining her in guarding Cassandra, including Dakota and Duncan.

I nod to each wolf as I pass them on the way to the occupied bedroom. Once inside, I shift to human. "Is there any reason the council would've told the vampires about what I am?"

Cassandra shakes her head. "I don't see why they would. There's a small subset of vampires who would like nothing more than to wipe werewolves out of existence. If word got out to any of them about your strengths as a hybrid, they might come after you, thinking you could somehow help them achieve that goal. Suffice it to say that's not something the witches would want to risk."

Although I already suspected the witches weren't involved, my stomach sinks. I reach for her hand. "Everything will be all right," I say, but the words are more for me than her.

I strain my ears, but whatever is happening in the woods is too far away for me to hear. Maybe this is good. Maybe the pack is chasing the vampires away.

My skin tingles. Something's wrong, but I can't

place what.

"I'll be right back," I murmur before standing and shifting back to wolf form. When I walk out, I address Maggie, Dakota, and Duncan. *Do you guys sense anything strange?*

A chorus of *no*s sounds in my head, but I'm not convinced something odd isn't happening. The invaders are out in the woods where the rest of the pack is, but I can't shake the feeling that danger is still headed our way. But if there are vampires close to us, we should be able to smell them.

I'm about to go back in to sit with Cassandra when the plate glass window at the front of the house shatters. Two vampires leap in among the shards. The one with the unnaturally light blond hair and amber eyes is Xander. The shoulder-length dark brown hair of the other man is pulled back into a low ponytail. Although I don't know his name, I recognize him from the same place I know Xander from: Luke's mansion.

A weight settles in my chest, pressing the air from my lungs. I was right—Luke must have figured out what I am and told his brood. It's my fault they're here now.

Xander takes a step toward us, the motion greeted by growls. "I know you dogs can understand me, so I'll tell it to you plain: Give me the hybrid."

None of us move, and he leers before nodding

at his companion. "Okay, the hard way it is. Carlos, how about you persuade these mutts to give us the one we want?"

Carlos pulls a knife from a sheath on his belt buckle. Even if it weren't obvious from the thick rubber grip on the handle, the scent would give away what it's made of: silver. I get the sinking sensation I know what their plan is, but something doesn't make sense. How would they know silver won't hurt me the way it does other immortals?

Carlos takes a step toward Maggie and I growl. I don't know whether he plans to cut her or simply touch the blade to her skin, but either way, I have no intention of letting him get near her. Dakota and I dart forward at the same moment to act as a barrier. Carlos swipes at us with a knife, but Dakota lunges for his leg, clamping her jaw until I can hear the bones breaking. He yowls in pain, and I know what I have to do. I give into my wolf completely. She hates the idea of these invaders coming onto our territory, but the thing that angers her most is the fact that they would attempt to hurt Maggie. I need to protect her, at all costs.

I jump up and clamp my jaw closed around Carlos's neck. Dakota pulls at his legs, and together we manage to separate his head from his body.

I look up in time to see Xander and Duncan locked in battle. I'm about to spring in to help, but

Xander is too fast. He strikes out with a silver knife of his own and cuts Duncan across his shoulder. Before he can do more damage, howling cuts through the air. More wolves are on the way.

Xander backs up, glaring at the four of us. "Make no mistake: I'll be back for the hybrid. And next time, she's mine." He slashes at the air with his knife one last time before turning and running as fast as he can out of the house. Through the hole where the window used to be, I watch Sawyer and a few other wolves give chase, but Xander is already too far away.

From the other room, Cassandra calls my name. Dakota and Maggie go to check on Duncan, and I shift to human before entering Cassandra's room.

She holds her hand toward me and I cross to take it. "Is everyone all right?"

I nod. "Two of them broke in here. One is dead, and the other ran off. We're all safe."

She purses her lips. "I very much doubt that."

My back straightens and I sniff the air tentatively, but I don't smell anything out of the ordinary. Then again, I didn't realize Xander and Carlos were nearby until they crashed into the living room.

She nods as if reading my thoughts. "Please arrange for me to examine the dead vampire," she says, struggling to prop herself into a sitting position.

I bite my lower lip. “I don’t think Jack will like that.”

Her eyebrows hike upward. “Unfortunately, it doesn’t matter whether or not he’ll like it. It needs to be done.” She sighs. “I don’t know exactly what’s going on, but I get the feeling things just got much more complicated.”

A presence tugs at the back of my mind. Jack is drawing near to the enclave. “Yeah,” I agree softly. “And I think they’re about to get worse.”

CHAPTER TWENTY-TWO

JACK PACES back and forth in the living room of my house. His footfalls are heavy and deliberate, and he shakes the floor with each step, but at least he's stopped swearing.

After leaving Dakota with instructions to help Cassandra in any way possible, I met Jack on his way back to Maggie's house. I convinced him to follow me back to my place and dropped the bomb about my run-in with Luke as soon as he crossed the threshold. "I'm sorry I didn't tell you last night," I say again.

He stops and turns to stare at me. "Why didn't you?"

I sigh heavily. "I was afraid you were going to react like this."

"Like what?"

I throw up my hands. "Crazy?" I offer. "Jealous?"

He clenches his jaw. "I'm not jealous. I'm just angry because you kept it from me."

I cross my arms over my chest. "I get that. And if it was some random vampire I'd run into, I probably would've told you. But I get the sense there's some major history between you and Luke." I study his face. "Am I wrong about that?"

For a second he's silent; then he releases a heavy sigh and crosses to the couch where I'm sitting. He drops to the cushion beside me, resting his elbows on his knees. "Yes, we have history. I've been following Luke around, keeping tabs on him, since before I was turned. He's the first vampire I ever encountered."

I allow the information to sink in. "He's the reason you became a hunter."

He nods. "I knew the kind of monster he was, the horrors he was capable of. But things were no different then than they are now. No one believed immortals existed. I thought since I knew the truth, it was my responsibility to protect innocent people from the demons that hid in plain sight." A dark expression flickers across his face. "I only regret not having killed Luke before now. If I had, you wouldn't be in this situation to begin with. You'd be a wolf, not a hybrid, and you wouldn't be in danger."

I cover his hand with mine. "Do you believe in fate?" I ask. When he doesn't answer, I continue. "I never really did before, but since I found out I'm your half, I've been thinking more about it. Maybe it's fate that I am what I am."

He shakes his head, turning his hand over so our palms press together. "I don't want to believe it. If it's fate that you're a hybrid, then it's fate that we're in this situation, and I can't accept that."

I want to tell him more—how if I hadn't met Luke that night at the bar, I wouldn't have stayed out so late. If I hadn't been out so late, I wouldn't have been stabbed, and Jack probably would have continued watching me from afar. If he never had a reason to come near me, I may not have turned at all. But before I can make sense of the thoughts swirling in my head, his phone rings. Lillie's name flashes on the display.

Jack answers it and taps the button to put it on speaker. "What's going on?"

"Cassandra wants to talk," Lillie says.

Jack is on his feet immediately. The two of us run to Maggie's house. I'm surprised to see the broken window has been boarded up in our short absence. Jack is tense the whole way, even though there was nothing in Lillie's tone to indicate a problem.

Cassandra's face is pale and drawn when we

enter her room. Jack sucks in a breath. She looks much worse than she did when I left her. "I know what happened," she says, her voice scratchy.

Jack and I take spots on either side of her mattress. "What are you talking about?" he asks.

"I checked over the body of the dead vampire, and there's no mistaking what I sensed. There was a concealment charm cast over him." She leans back onto the pillows propped against her headboard.

Jack stands, cursing. "You should be focusing all your energy on getting better."

"*Calme-toi, Jacques,*" she murmurs. "We need to know who we're up against."

"I already know who we're up against," Jack growls. "I recognized some of the leeches at the perimeter. I saw them at the mansion the day I went to rescue Ava. He was lurking just beyond our territory last night, and he must've figured out what Ava is when he talked with her. It's Luke."

"You can't believe that," she says, her voice stronger.

"Like it's such a stretch."

I'm taken aback by the venom in his voice. Why does Jack hate him so much?

Cassandra lifts her hand, and the motion is enough to make Jack sit back down. "Why? Why would Luke want Ava?"

"I can think of a few reasons," he mutters

darkly.

She exhales noisily. “You know my stance, and I won’t waste breath trying to convince you to see things differently than you do, but trust me when I say I don’t think Luke has anything to do with this.”

“It doesn’t really matter who’s behind it,” I say. “What matters is we make sure no one attacks our territory again. You said there was a concealment charm on Carlos. Is there any way of telling who did it?”

Cassandra shakes her head. “If I weren’t so weak, maybe—but only if I were familiar with the witch in question. It’s possible these vampires compelled some weaker-minded witches to do the spellwork for them.”

“What’s the alternative?” I ask.

She and Jack trade glances. “They have a witch working with them. And if that’s the case, it changes things. Why vampires might want you is fairly straightforward—either to kill you so you can’t make a stronger force to keep them in check, or replicate you to create their own battalion to destroy the wolves.”

Both options make my stomach twist, but I nod. “And what would witches want with me?” I force a smile. “I mean, besides to kill me.”

Cassandra stretches out her arm and covers my hand with hers. “That’s what worries me. I have no idea."

CHAPTER TWENTY-THREE

IT'S BEEN TWO DAYS since Xander infiltrated our territory, and I'm watching Jack, Sawyer, Duncan, and a few others put the finishing touches on the new window that's going in to Maggie's house when I sense it. It isn't an intrusion—that would make my skin prickle and my hair stand on end. This is something different. A presence just beyond where our land ends.

He's waiting for me. I'm not sure how I know, but I can't deny it.

Luke.

The desire to go to him is strong, but not overpowering. Not yet, anyway. Lillie, who came out of the house about ten minutes ago to make sure the guys were hydrated and stayed to chat with me, raises an eyebrow. "You okay?"

I realize my mouth is hanging open and snap it closed. Why would Luke be here? Despite what Jack believes, I haven't been able to accept the idea that Luke was involved in the attack. But what if I was wrong? Perhaps he's employing a different tactic—a more gentle touch. Maybe he thinks I'll go to him and leave without putting up a fight. If that's the case, I don't think his pull on me is as strong as he believes.

It's hard to tell from this distance, but I think he's alone. Beyond the reaches of our territory, it becomes exponentially harder to determine who's nearby. I'm certain the only reason I can feel Luke's presence at all is due to the sire bond.

"I have to talk to Jack," I say, already stepping away from Lillie's side.

His eyebrows draw together as I approach him. He hands the caulk gun to Duncan and stands. "What's wrong?"

I take his hand and pull him down the porch stairs and around to the side of the house. By the time I stop walking, he's smiling. "I haven't been at work that long, have I? If you needed me to take a break, you should've just said something." He slides a hand around the back of my neck and steps in like he's ready to give me a kiss, but I duck away.

"It's not that." I hesitate. Not telling him immediately about my last encounter only angered him. Still, I don't want him to overreact before we know what's happening. "Do you... feel anything strange?"

"Besides confusion about why you're acting this way? No." He stoops to catch my eye. "What's going on?"

I bite my lower lip. "I'm going to tell you something, but you have to promise to stay calm—at least until we know what's going on."

It was the wrong thing to say. Jack's playful demeanor from moments ago evaporates, replaced by coiled tension and anger simmering just beneath the surface. "What are you talking about? Tell me."

At this point, the last thing I want to do is tell Jack what I'm sensing, but I have to. "Luke. He's nearby. Not in the territory, but close to it."

Jack curses. "His friends didn't do enough damage the other day?"

I hold up my hands. "I can't tell why he's here. But I think we should go check it out."

He nods. "I'll get a group together and—"

I shake my head. "If he wanted to hurt us, he could've just used one of the charms Xander had and snuck in here. He's not on our territory, but I think he wants me to know he's close. I think I should go out to see what he wants."

A muscle in his jaw jumps, and there's a steely glint in his eye. "I don't want you near him by yourself."

I arch an eyebrow. "I could say the same thing about you." When he shoots me a wounded look, I press on. "I get that you two have some kind of history. I get that you hate him. But now isn't the time to go killing him without a reason."

"I have plenty of reasons," Jack growls.

I place my hands on his arms. "Let's just go see what he wants. You and me. We can keep each other in check." I offer a small smile, which Jack doesn't return.

After a beat, he nods. "I'm going to let Dakota and the betas know what we're up to. I want them to be on alert just in case Luke is here as some kind of distraction."

"Of course," I agree, even though my gut tells me it isn't necessary. Maybe it's just the sire bond, but I have the feeling that Luke isn't here to hurt me. I shake my head. It's ridiculous. Probably just wishful thinking. All evidence points to him knowing what I am. Why else would members of his brood show up to try to take me away the day after I saw him in the woods?

Jack's voice echoes in my head as he sends a message to Dakota, Sawyer, and Cecily. He tells them what's going on and to be on guard. He adds that reinforcements should be ready to meet us if anyone senses an intrusion on pack lands. I think the measures are unnecessary, but I keep it to myself.

Once he's done communicating, Jack nods, indicating I should lead the way. We shift as we begin running. It's strange to me that he can't sense Luke's presence when it sticks out like a beacon to me.

We slow as we near the edge of the territory. By now Luke's scent is strong, and I know Jack must be able to smell him. At Jack's prompting, I shift back to human; we're still too deep in the woods to be seen from the two-lane road just beyond the edge of our territory. A car is parked on the shoulder, and Luke leans against the hood. He's staring in our direction when we emerge from the trees.

Jack positions himself between Luke and me before shifting. "Don't come any closer. My weres have orders to kill anyone who enters the territory," he says, his voice low.

Luke holds up his hands innocently. "You'll notice I was careful not to step foot onto your land. I come in peace."

I cross my arms over my chest. "I'm not sure I believe you."

He glances pointedly at Jack. "I assume his influence has something to do with that."

"Why are you here?" Jack asks, his voice heavy with alpha authority. Even though it doesn't have the same effect on vampires, I can't help thinking anyone who heard him would be influenced to some extent.

But Luke seems impervious. He surveys Jack for a moment longer before sighing, his shoulders slumping slightly. "I've come to offer my help."

Jack snorts, throwing up his hands. "I knew this was a waste of time. Ava, let's go back to the enclave."

I'm more than a little surprised by Jack's reaction. How can he be so ready to dismiss Luke's offer? I get the feeling vampires and werewolves don't often team up, so I'm not willing to leave before I know what brought Luke here, and why he thinks we need his assistance. "Let's hear him out."

Jack's eyes are fixed on Luke, and I wonder if he heard me. "Let me guess: Some of your leech friends are stationed somewhere just outside my territory. You were hoping I'd come with my strongest fighters and leave Ava alone so they could try to make a grab for her again. Offering help—this is what? Plan B? Are you waiting for backup?"

Luke's gaze flickers to me. "Again? Someone came after you?"

I take a half step forward, nodding. "Yes. Xander and Carlos, and I don't know how many others from your brood."

He curses, and I catch a flicker of doubt in

Jack's eye. "I smelled magic on Xander the other day, but he swore he'd bumped into a witch in town completely by accident." He runs a hand through his blond hair, causing it to stick up the way Jack's sometimes does. The similarity is so striking it takes me a moment to process what he says next. "I should've put it together sooner. I should've figured out something was wrong when people first started going missing."

My eyebrows hike up. "Wait—missing? Who's been going missing?"

Jack is standing at attention, too. "I thought you said your brood wasn't breaking our deal?"

Luke holds out a hand. "Down, boy. I wasn't lying."

"That'd be a first," Jack mutters.

Luke ignores him. "After your assault on the mansion, some members of the brood went out one night and didn't come back."

"I'm surprised you noticed," Jack murmurs.

Luke shrugs. "One of them owed me money."

"So, some of your housemates didn't come home. What's the big deal?" I ask. "I didn't think vampires were family the way weres are."

"Family." Luke says the word like a curse, glaring at Jack. "I suppose he's been teaching you all about what family means, hasn't he?"

"She asked you a question," Jack snaps, his tone

sharper than strictly necessary.

Luke smirks, as if he's pleased to have hit a nerve. "I didn't think much of it at first," he continues after a beat. "Things at the mansion are always in flux. People come and go pretty regularly. But then another pair went missing."

"Maybe they didn't want to run the risk of the pack coming back," I offer. It seems a plausible reason to me.

"When it comes to most of the vampires I know, I'd agree with you. But Dinah was one of the last ones not to come back, and that's not like her at all. If she were taking off, there's no way she'd leave her shoes behind." He drops his gaze and rubs the back of his neck. "Girl was obsessed with her designer shoes."

"Was?" I ask.

He meets my eyes. "I started poking around. I went into town and checked some places she liked to hang out." The corners of his mouth quirk. "Compelled a few people into recalling details they otherwise wouldn't have remembered. And then I found it." His nose twitches and he rubs it absently. "Smelled it, really. The stench... I'm surprised the humans living in the apartments nearby hadn't complained."

The hairs on the back of my neck stand up and a weight sinks in my stomach. I don't want to hear this. "The stench?"

"Bodies," he says unceremoniously. "The vampires from my brood. In a dumpster."

"I'm sorry for your loss," I murmur, but Jack talks over me.

"How'd they die?"

Luke crosses his arms over his chest. "That's the interesting part. If I didn't know any better, I'd swear they'd been bitten by a wolf."

"It wasn't us," Jack says immediately. "No one in my pack would do something like that."

"Believe it or not, I didn't come to accuse you of anything," Luke says. "After I found them, I remembered something I'd overheard at the house. Xander tried to play it off like he was talking about a car engine, but..." He shakes his head. "He said something about a hybrid."

My muscles tense and Jack clenches his jaw. Luke takes no notice of either reaction.

"Let me save you time—I know they meant Ava." He shakes his head. "It's so obvious, looking back. When Jack showed up to take you away, I figured he was just being a douche. More punishment for past sins and all that. And when I saw you in the woods—I could smell the wolf on you, but I figured it was because you were spending time with them. But after I found the bodies the way I did, it all made sense. Somehow, that's what you are. And someone's trying to make more like you."

"Not me," I say quickly. "I don't want to make any more. I wouldn't even know how."

"Obviously neither does whoever's doing this." Luke's gaze flickers to Jack. "It's Xander—it has to be. And it seems he's working with at least one witch."

"But that doesn't make any sense," I say. "The witches at the council were afraid I'd try to make more. Why would they go and try it themselves?"

"I don't know," Jack says, taking a step closer to me. "And it's possible Xander and his companions are compelling someone to do their dirty work. Still, we need to tell Cassandra."

Luke's eyebrows hitch upward. "Cassie's with you in wolf world?"

It's my turn to be surprised. While Cassandra seemed to have an idea who Luke was, I figured it was because Jack had mentioned him before. "Wait—you know Cassandra?"

He doesn't look at me. "You haven't told her, have you? I don't know why I'm surprised."

I turn to Jack. "Haven't told me what?"

Jack ignores me. "Thanks for letting us know what's going on. I'll make sure Ava's safe." He turns back toward the territory, but before he can take more than a step, Luke is at his side, spinning him until they face each other.

"That's it? You're just going to run back to your little campground and—what? Hide under a table and hope the next time Xander or someone else comes looking for her they don't notice where she is?" He presses in close until his face is just inches from Jack's. "How long do you think it'll be before Xander's back with reinforcements? You need to get her out of here. Hide her somewhere the witches won't be able to track her."

"Believe it or not, we can't just pick up and leave at the drop of a hat. Wolves are territorial; we can't just set up camp somewhere new on a whim."

"Really?" Luke's tone is dubious. "Because you've been following my ass around for the better part of a century. Territorial lines never seemed to bother you before."

I don't bother hiding my surprise. I knew Luke was the first vampire Jack ever came across, but he kept tabs on him all this time? If Jack hates him so much, why would he chase him around for so long?

Jack's shoulders slump. "I know some alphas of other packs—ones I trust. Someone might be willing to take us in until we can sort things out."

A satisfied smirk curves Luke's lips. "You'd better get on that. And be sure to let them know to make room for three."

Jack takes a step backward, incredulity spreading across his face. "Only two of us are going."

"Really? I wasn't thinking you were going to want to hang back." Luke narrows his eyes. "Whether you like it or not, I'm coming. You can't tell me my venom isn't in her. I'm as responsible for her being what she is as you are. What makes you think I don't want to make sure she's safe?"

"Let's just say your track record speaks for itself."

Luke's eyes flash red and he reaches for Jack, but before he can make contact, I jump between them. He sneers as his irises return to their usual shade of electric blue. "What's this? Big bad alpha can't fight his own battles?"

My wolf takes the insult personally. She doesn't like that her partner's strength is being challenged. "Not at all," I snap. "I just don't like the idea of standing by while someone tries to grab my half."

I wasn't planning to say it, and it's clear by the way Luke tenses that he wasn't expecting to hear it. His gaze flickers to Jack's face. "She's your..."

"Half," Jack says, sliding his hand protectively around my abdomen.

Luke takes in a deep breath and releases it slowly. "*Félicitations, Jacques,*" he murmurs.

Jack sighs, and some of the tension in his muscles drains. "*Merci, Luc.*"

I step from between them, legitimately baffled.

I've heard Cassandra call Jack *Jacques* before, but it's the way he says Luke's name that I can't wrap my mind around. The vowel sound is rounder, but that's not all that's different. The tone of his voice is entirely changed, like he's speaking to a dear friend, not a vampire he appears to loathe.

"Okay, what's going on?" I demand.

Luke quirks an eyebrow. "We're speaking French. A language spoken in the European country of—"

I wave my hand dismissively. "I know you're speaking French. What I can't figure out is why you decided to switch from English, or why you both sound..." I grasp for the right words. "Why you suddenly sound like you care about each other. Were you two friends once a hundred years ago or something?"

Luke sighs. "Are you going to tell her, or should I?"

Jack runs a hand through his hair, his shoulders slumping. "Friends? Not exactly. Luke is my brother."

CHAPTER TWENTY-FOUR

IT TAKES a considerable amount of time for me to come to terms with what Jack has told me.

Brothers. Luke and Jack are *brothers*.

The more I think about it, the more it begins to make sense. Despite the superficial differences in their appearance—Jack's darker hair and complexion versus Luke's fairer skin and hair—the two bear resemblances. Their builds are similar—muscular, with broad shoulders and slim waists. Their jaws have the same curve. Their eyes even crinkle in the same way when they smile.

I watch the way the two of them move as we walk through the forest back to the enclave after Jack alerts the pack about our visitor. The way they duck around branches is nearly identical, and I can't believe I didn't realize the two were related before now.

No one speaks until we're about halfway back to the enclave. Dakota, Sawyer, and a handful of other weres stand in a line, their bodies tense like they're ready to spring into action in case their alpha was under duress when he indicated he'd be bringing a vampire to our home. Jack holds up a hand. "It's fine," he says, and the group visibly relaxes. "Luke is the one who bit Ava, and he came to tell us she's in trouble."

"Which we already knew," Dakota says. She won't make a move against Luke, but it's obvious from the look in her eye she'd like to. Still, she respects Jack's authority.

"And he's willing to help protect her," Jack adds, the additional information causing those assembled to murmur with surprise. "He'll be sequestered until we have a plan. Dakota, I want to meet wit you and the betas at the meeting house in ten minutes—after I get Luke situated."

"I can't wait," Luke says drily. "Garlic-soaked ropes, a cage with silver bars. Is that about right?"

"Something like that," Jack grumbles.

I can't believe what I'm hearing. "You can't lock him up like he's some kind of prisoner. He's—" I bite back what I want to say. "Our guest."

He raises his eyebrows like he knows exactly which words I wanted to use. "He may have our conditional trust, but I won't put the rest of the pack in a situation where they feel unsafe."

"I'll watch him," I say immediately.

A muscle in his jaw jumps. He doesn't like the idea—I can see it in his eyes—but after a moment, he relents. "Fine. But I'm posting a guard outside your house."

A smile spreads across Luke's face. "You afraid she and I are going to pick up where we left off last time we were alone?"

Jack growls, but I'm faster. I round on him and give him a quick jab in the stomach, the way Sawyer has been teaching me. Luke doubles over, his breath escaping in a loud gush.

"Whoa," he says when he's able to stand straight again. "Stronger than you look, aren't you?"

I can't quite suppress my smile as I turn to Jack. "Pretty sure I can take care of myself, should it come to that."

Jack doesn't look entirely convinced, but he nods. "I'm still stationing guards."

I step in close and rise up on my tiptoes to meet his lips. "I would expect nothing less."

I'm about to plant my heels again when Jack circles me with one strong arm and pulls me to him again. When our lips meet this time, my whole body tingles. I know there are things to be done, plans to be made, but for the moment, all those tasks fade into the back of my mind. The only thing that matters is Jack and the way he makes me feel. I wish we could stay like this forever. Too quickly, Jack releases me, and calls for Duncan and Angela to accompany Luke and me.

The weres keep their distance as I lead the way to my house. I'm not sure if they're trying to give the two of us privacy or whether they're simply uncomfortable being so close to a vampire.

"Thank you," I say as we walk along the dirt road.

"For what?" He kicks at some gravel, sending it skittering along ahead of us.

"Coming to help me. You didn't have to do that."

He raises an eyebrow. "I don't want you operating under the false assumption that my presence here is entirely altruistic. Members of my brood are showing up dead. If I can help you stop whoever's trying to make more hybrids, it decreases my chances of ending up face down in a dumpster."

"Oh." I bite my lower lip. I don't know what I was expecting. I suppose I've grown so accustomed to Jack's unconditional protection that I took for granted that Luke might have his own reasons for wanting to help.

We come to the bend in the road and I nod up at the cabin that's become my home. "There's my place."

The corners of his mouth quirk. "Let me guess: The one on top of the hill is Jack's."

I nod and Luke gives a soft snort.

Duncan and Angela elect to stay out on the porch when Luke and I go inside. As he takes a seat on the couch, I can't help remembering the way it felt when he kissed me in the mansion. A shiver travels down my spine, but I shake it off.

Even though I'm not thirsty, I go to the kitchen for a glass of water. I feel Luke's eyes on me the whole time. "So," I ask as I turn on the tap, "how'd you die?" It's not until after the question is in the air that I realize it might have been inappropriate. While he asked me the same thing, circumstances were a bit different since he knew me when I was still alive.

I fill the glass and turn off the water, but he doesn't speak until I'm back in the living room. "Consumption. You know—tuberculosis? Big-time killer back in the day." The corners of his mouth quirk up. "There were rumors of a woman who could heal any illness, and my—" His lips twitch and his gaze drops for a moment. "Suffice it to say she wasn't really a healer."

I nod, sorry I brought it up. Still, I can't help wanting to press further. While I've learned more about who Jack is, I still know so little about his past. How much does Luke know? Were the two of them close when they were both still human? Jack said Luke is the reason he became a hunter—but why would Jack want to hunt his own brother?

Somehow, it feels like learning these things from Luke wouldn't mean as much as hearing them from Jack. Instead, I settle on another question I've had since before we came back to the enclave. "How do you know Cassandra?"

Luke shakes his head. "Wow. Jack really hasn't told you anything, has he?"

I bristle. "Of course he's told me things." I find myself wanting to defend Jack, despite the fact that there are clearly a host of details he's been keeping from me. In a way, it hurts, but I suppose if I had more than a hundred years of life experience, there would be too much for me to share all at once.

He surveys me for another moment, rubbing the back of his neck. "I know Cassie the same way Jack does—or at least for the same reason. She's our cousin."

I can't hide my shock. "No."

"Yes. I mean, close enough, you know? Our father's brother married a witch. Cassie's their granddaughter. I met her one day completely by chance." He smiles at the memory. "I tried to compel her to give me her horse and she stared me in the eye and told me no. It was the first time I'd come across a witch—or anyone—strong enough to resist my compulsion. She knew what I was, but she wasn't afraid. She'd heard of vampires, of course, but she'd never met one. She wanted to understand me, so she invited me back to her house for a meal."

Somehow, I have no problem imagining a much younger Cassandra demanding Luke tell her all about his kind. "When did you figure out you were related?"

He shrugs. "It came up in conversation."

While it's not exactly an answer, I don't press. "So the two of you are close, huh?" I ask instead. When his eyebrows draw together, I add, "You called her 'Cassie.' I figure if you've got a nickname for her, you must be close."

"It was a long time ago."

I bite my lower lip. More similarities between Jack and Luke are presenting themselves, although I suppose it's possible a tendency to under-share is more a consequence of being immortal than of blood relation. "If you'd like to go see her, I could arrange it."

"I don't think Jack would like that very much."

Indignation swells in my chest. I don't need to run every decision by Jack. He may be my alpha, but he doesn't control me. "If Cassandra wants to see you, it doesn't matter if Jack likes it."

The coldness in my voice gives me pause. Why

am I getting so worked up? Adrenaline courses through my veins. I feel ready to start a fight at the slightest provocation.

Something Cassandra mentioned about the sire bond between vampires floats to the surface of my mind, and I look at Luke. "What are you doing to me?"

"What do you mean?" he asks, but I easily detect his feigned innocence.

I set my water glass on the nearest counter before stalking toward him, my finger in the air like a parent issuing a warning. "Obviously you and Jack have a ton of history I know nothing about. That doesn't give you the right to project those feelings onto me. He's my half, and I—" I stop short, not entirely sure how to put my feelings for Jack into words. When Luke lifts his eyebrows, I continue, "I care about him—a lot. And I don't want you getting in my head and making me think otherwise."

He covers my hand with his and gently pushes it out of his face. "Believe it or not, I wasn't trying to make you think anything. This sire bond thing is a new experience for me too, you know."

The fight goes out of me and I sit on the cushion beside him. "You mean I'm the first person you ever turned?"

"No. But there haven't been many." He leans

back, lacing his fingers behind his head. "No use having a harem of lovesick women following me around for all eternity."

I cross my arms over my chest and roll my eyes. "Is that what you think of me?"

He shakes his head. "I don't know what to think of you."

His electric blue eyes lock on mine, and for a moment my brain refuses to work. I can't think through the heavy fog clouding my mind. Luke is the only thing in the world, and part of me wants to lose myself in him forever, but something in the back of my mind stops me. This isn't right. I don't want Luke—not like this.

I stand, covering my face with my hands. Whatever weight had been pressing down on me dissipates, leaving my mind clear. Once I've collected myself, I drop my arms to my sides. Staring across the room at the glass of water, I ask, "So, do you want to see Cassandra or not?"

CHAPTER TWENTY-FIVE

LILLIE PULLS ME into a hug so tight it's hard for me to breathe. "I'll be back before you know it," I say. My assurance only makes her pull me closer.

It's only been a couple of hours since Jack and I returned to the enclave with Luke, and already the three of us are preparing to leave. Jack was able to find a sympathetic friend who will give us a safe place to stay—at least until we can figure out our next move. Now, Jack is in Cassandra's room, bidding her farewell, I imagine. He wanted a few minutes alone with her. Luke lingers by the front door, a disgruntled look marring his features. He spent the better part of the last hour catching up with Cassandra and was none too pleased when Jack arrived and kicked him out.

Maggie eyes him warily as she displaces Lillie

to embrace me. "We'll take good care of Cassandra while you're gone," she murmurs.

"I know you will," I say.

Before either of us can go on, the bedroom door swings open and Jack emerges, his expression clouded. He glances at me before jerking his head toward the front of the house. "Let's get going."

While I'd like the chance to say goodbye to Cassandra myself, I understand we're on a schedule. I join him as he walks through the house toward his brother, but he doesn't reach for the doorknob. Jack holds out his hand; resting in the center of his palm are three small bags suspended from silky black cords. Although I can't see through the black fabric, I smell the mix of herbs inside.

"You shouldn't have let her make these," he grumbles as Luke and I each take one of the charms. "She's too weak to be working magic. She needs to devote all her energy to getting better."

Luke snorts. "You know her just as well as I do—probably better. No one *lets* Cassie do anything."

"What are these for?" I ask, slipping the necklace over my head.

Jack stops staring daggers at his brother long enough to answer my question. "She says this is the same magic that made it possible for Xander and his friends to sneak into the enclave without us detecting him. She thinks these will help us get to where we're going without anyone noticing we're on the move."

"She thinks?" Luke asks, cocking an eyebrow. "Since when is she unsure about her magical abilities?"

"In all the time you spent with her just now, did you somehow miss how weak she is?" Jack snaps.

I step between them. "Boys," I say, doing my best imitation of a teacher attempting to diffuse a fight. "We should probably get a move on."

Jack closes his eyes and exhales through his nose before leading the way out to the SUV in front of the house. Lillie and Maggie wave from the porch as the three of us climb in.

Buckles click as Jack and I fasten our belts. He peers in the rearview mirror at Luke. "Put on your seatbelt," he says as he puts the car in reverse to pull onto the road.

"What part of *immortal* don't you understand?" Luke asks, making no move to comply.

Jack starts up the road that will take us out of the enclave. "I'm not looking for a reason to get pulled over today."

Luke shrugs. "If someone tries, just pull over, and I'll compel him to let us drive away."

Jack slams on the brakes and Luke jolts

forward, his head banging against the back of my seat. “Buckle up,” Jack says as his brother curses.

I can’t quite cover up my snort of laughter. “Let me guess,” I say as I hear the click of a seatbelt in the back seat, “Jack is the older brother?”

“You guessed wrong,” Luke grumbles.

The next few minutes pass in silence. It isn’t until we merge onto the freeway that Luke speaks up. “Are we going to drive all the way to wherever it is we’re going?” When Jack doesn’t respond, he continues, “What? I’m not allowed to ask questions?”

I stare at Jack’s profile. I know the plan only in broad strokes, but I could answer the question myself. Still, something stops me. I need to know whether Jack actually trusts his brother or if Luke is here only at my insistence.

As if he can feel my gaze on him, Jack glances at me. He releases a sigh. “It’d take too long by car. We’re flying.”

“You really think now is the time for commercial air travel?” Luke scoffs.

“I assume the pack has its own plane,” I say. This part of the plan is nebulous even to me.

Jack sighs. “We do, but it’s not exactly a secret. It’s too big a risk to assume Xander or whoever’s after Ava wouldn’t be watching it. My friend is sending his pack’s plane to pick us up at an airfield in neutral territory."

"It's not the worst plan I've ever heard," Luke says. "Maybe you're not as stupid as you look, little brother."

Jack growls, and I get the feeling if he weren't driving, his reaction might have been a little more forceful. Has their relationship always been strained? Jack told me he became a hunter because he knew what kinds of horrors vampires were capable of. What could Luke have done to make his own brother see him as a monster?

No one speaks until we arrive at a small airfield less than an hour later. It's late afternoon, and people dot the area. My body tenses involuntarily each time we pass a person or a car, but no one seems to be paying us any notice. I crack the window and sniff the breeze as we go, but everyone we pass smells human. I try to tell myself that means we're safe, that our plan will work, but my muscles remain coiled.

Jack pulls to a stop by a runway toward the back of the airfield. He checks the time on the dashboard. "They should be here soon."

My eyes flick to the sky. I've never ridden on a plane before, and the thought of being a passenger on one of the small ones we've been driving by makes my stomach churn. Maybe it's ridiculous. Air travel is supposed to be super-safe, and even if we were to crash, I get the feeling I would survive the impact.

I can't help wondering what Xander and his minions are up to now. Why on earth would he want to make more hybrids like me? Does he hope to make himself stronger and impervious to many threats the way I am, or are his aims different? Darker?

"There it is," Jack says, pointing at a small plane still high in the air. He climbs out of the car, and Luke and I follow suit. We will figure everything out. Jack told me his friend's territory is in the Upper Peninsula. It's far enough away that we won't have to be constantly on guard against attack. We'll be able to devote all our time to figuring out what Xander's end goal is.

The plane touches down and taxis to a stop. When the door opens, Jack walks to greet the man who exits. He is huge—probably at least six foot six—and even if I didn't know he was a werewolf, his physical presence would be intimidating. His dark hair is long and wild, but his smile is jovial when his eyes land on Jack.

"Chet," Jack says, embracing the man when his feet hit the tarmac. "It's been a long time, my friend."

"Indeed it has," Chet replies. He glances over Jack's shoulder, his eyes narrowing when he sees

Luke. “Interesting company you’re keeping these days.”

“Don’t I know it,” Jack grumbles. “That’s Luke,” he says dismissively as he crosses to my side. “And this is Ava.”

Chet moves cautiously as he approaches me, and I sense hesitation when he extends his hand. I take it and hold it firmly. My dad instilled in me the importance of a solid handshake. “It’s nice to meet you,” I say, and I mean it. “Thank you for helping us.”

The corners of Chet’s mouth quirk upward as he releases my hand. “When Jack first told me what you were, I couldn’t believe it. Even now, with you here in front of me, I’m having a hard time wrapping my head around it.”

“You’re not the only one,” I say. I mean it to come out lighthearted, like a joke, but the words hang heavily in the air between us.

He turns his attention to Luke. “Never thought I’d live to see the day when werewolves and vampires were working together side by side.”

“I know it’s strange,” Jack says, cutting off whatever Luke was thinking of saying. “But we can trust him.”

Chet releases a heavy sigh. “The fact that you actually believe that is all I need to be sure I’m doing the right thing.”

Warning bells go off in my head, but before any of us can react, half a dozen wolves from Chet's pack leap from the plane, never setting a paw on the stairs. "Grab the hybrid!"

"Run!" Jack yells.

I don't think—I react. I could shift—I'm moderately faster in that form—but I don't think that's my best option right now. While we are in neutral territory, that doesn't mean Chet doesn't have contact with nearby packs. If I run blind into the woods, how long before I cross into someone else's territory? There's no guarantee there aren't weres already waiting for me.

I run back to the SUV we arrived in. If I'm honest, I don't know how its top speed compares to that of most wolves, but at least inside I'll have an added layer of protection.

It's not until I'm behind the wheel that I realize Jack and Luke aren't following. The two of them are doing their best to keep the attackers from getting to me. The keys are in the ignition and I start the engine, but a flicker of indecision keeps me from putting the car in gear. I don't want to leave them.

I don't have a choice. I slam the car into drive and press on the accelerator. The tires squeal as I make a tight circle to face the exit. I clutch the steering wheel to keep myself firmly in the driver's seat. In the back of my mind, I hear Jack's voice warning me to put on my seatbelt, but I can't yet—I need to put more distance between me and the attackers.

I slam on the gas pedal and a few howls rise up behind me—irritation at their prey eluding them. A glance in the rearview mirror is all I need to see that Jack and Luke are taking the momentary distraction to their advantage. The two of them take off at a run toward a line of trees a mile away from their position.

I sigh with relief as I turn my attention back to the road in front of me. They got away. Although I'm not entirely sure how, I'm confident I can meet up with them and together the three of us can formulate a new plan.

Why would Chet double-cross us? From the way Jack spoke with him, I got the feeling he trusted the man with his life. The two were even in the same pack for a number of years. What could possibly make him turn against his friend?

I turn out onto the main road. It's just a two-lane highway, but reaching it makes me feel better—safer—than I was while still on the airfield property.

There weren't many cars on the road on our way to the airfield, so I'm surprised to see three dark SUVs in my rearview mirror and two through my windshield. I inhale deeply, the scent spilling in through the cracked window putting me on alert.

Vampires.

Was Chet working with them? Or did they follow us?

One of the cars in front of me swerves into my lane. It's still half a mile up the road from me, but we're both traveling very fast. They're trying to block my escape.

I have a mind to play this game of chicken out, but I'm not entirely sure it's for the best. I've seen images of people whose heads were taken off when they careened through a windshield. There's no way I'd live through that.

At the last possible second, I jerk my wheel to the left and jam down on the accelerator. I intend to pull off the road only long enough to get around the oncoming car, but the terrain on the shoulder is looser than I anticipated, and the car goes skidding.

I brace for impact as I careen toward a thick tree trunk, but even my enhanced strength is no match for the force with which I hit it. The airbag deploys, but I'm going too fast. With no seatbelt to tether me to the seat, I shoot right through the windshield and collide with the tree.

I'm still conscious as I hit the ground, but blackness quickly creeps in on my periphery. I'm awake long enough to see all five cars pull to a stop on the shoulder. Several sets of feet hit the ground and come for me.

CHAPTER TWENTY-SIX

EVERYTHING ACHES. My whole body feels like it's on fire. Maybe I am on fire. I can't tell. I can't open my eyes.

What happened? There's a blank space in my memory. I was at a bar. No—that was weeks ago. Or was it last night?

No, time has passed. I got stabbed, I survived. I became a werewolf. But I'm more than that. I'm a hybrid. That's why people are after me.

My eyelids open a slit and I detect light. It's not very bright, but at least I know there will be something to see when I'm finally able to open my eyes. I focus my energy on my ears, hoping I might hear something to clue me in as to where I am, but everything is muffled. Maybe there are voices, or maybe it's just the sound of the wind whipping through the trees.

Some of the burning in my body subsides. Healing—that's what the feeling is. How badly was I hurt?

Images flash in my mind. I went through the windshield. Vampires were after me, and I tried to get away.

A heavy weight sinks in the bottom of my stomach. I don't think I did.

My chin is against my chest. I'm finally starting to get a sense of where my body is in space. I'm sitting up—in a chair. I try to move my arms and legs, but nothing happens.

"She's awake," says a male voice. His faint Southern drawl is familiar somehow, but I can't place it.

I direct all my energy to opening my eyes. I'm staring down at my legs, which are bound with thick ropes. Upon further inspection, I realize in addition to the ones binding my thighs, there are ropes around my ankles. My arms hang down at my sides and are tied to the legs of the chair. I pull against them, but my effort is wasted. They don't budge.

"Don't bother," says the same person who spoke a moment ago. "You may be strong, but I'm going to bet you can't break through Kevlar rope."

It takes two tries before I can pull my head up to center and focus on the speaker. As soon as I see his face, I know why he sounds so familiar. “Xander.”

He sweeps his hand and ducks his head in an odd kind of bow. “I told you next time you’d be mine.”

For the first time, I take in my surroundings. The room we’re in is large, but dark. It looks like a garage or warehouse that’s been repurposed into a makeshift home. Heavy curtains obscure the windows. Around the perimeter are large boxes covered with dark blankets. And we’re not alone. Other vampires peek at me curiously over the back of a couch that’s facing the same direction I am. Four of them sit together in the corner, one girl looking on as a second girl and two guys play a video game projected on a large flat-screen TV on the wall. The whole place smells musty.

“Why am I here? What do you want from me?”

Xander positions a metal folding chair about three yards from me and settles down on it. “You are a curiosity. I’ve been in plenty of scrapes with dogs in my time. They’ve bitten me, and I’ve bitten them, but neither of those things ever turned anyone into what you are.”

I shake my head. “I don’t know how I became a hybrid. So if you brought me here for the secret recipe, you’re out of luck.”

He leans forward, resting his elbows on his

knees. “See, at first I thought the same thing—that I needed to figure out how you came to be in order to replicate you. I acquired a werewolf to assist me and the two of us bit several people, but all of them died. I figured the process was too much for a human to handle, so I had my pet bite some vampires. Surely, I thought, their rapid healing would allow them to survive the change. But they were disappointments also.”

I attempt to rock side to side in the chair only to find it’s bolted to the ground. “Why does it matter? Why do you want to make more like me?”

He smirks. “Suffice it to say I’m tired of my every move being policed by dogs. If what I’ve heard is true, silver doesn’t bother you. While you were out, we tested your reaction to garlic and wolfsbane, and neither had an effect.”

“You want more hybrids so they can bully the werewolves for you?” I shake my head. “Hate to break it to you, but if they’re anything like me, they’ll side with the weres.”

He narrows his amber eyes. “I can be persuasive.”

I pull against my bindings. “Do you think Jack won’t come for me? If you don’t want him to kill you, you’d better let me go now!” But even as I say the words, doubt gathers in my mind. How will Jack find me? How long will the charm Cassandra made shield my location?

Xander holds up his hands innocently. "Believe it or not, I don't intend to keep you here forever, and I don't want to hurt you. I just need you to do something for me, and then you can be on your way. Run back to your werewolf or your vampire. Hell, run back to both of them—I won't judge."

My heart leaps at his mention of Jack and Luke. If I can run back to them, it must mean neither was captured or harmed when Xander caught me. I want nothing more than to get back to the enclave, to Jack, to my family. But am I willing to do Xander's bidding to get there? "Why would I help you?"

He reaches down to his ankle and raises his pants leg to reveal a small sheath from which he pulls a silver knife. "Because not helping me is a far less attractive option."

My stomach clenches, but I do my best to keep my face impassive. "You know silver isn't a poison to me like it is to you."

He raises his eyebrows. "Oh, it doesn't have to be poison to hurt."

Xander stands, his lips drawing back. His teeth glint in the low light. I hold my breath and gulp. He won't kill me. He wants me to do something for him, so he won't kill me.

The words repeat in my head as he closes the

distance between us. I grit my teeth, doing my best to prepare for what is about to happen, but when he stabs the blade into my abdomen, a scream rips itself from my throat.

BLOOD STAINS the ropes binding me to the chair and saturates the threadbare rug surrounding me. I must've lost consciousness. How long was I out?

I snap my head up and survey the room. The vampires in the corner are still playing a video game, and the drapes over the windows make it impossible to tell if there's been a change in the sun's position or intensity.

I'm not sure how long I've been here, but hours must have passed since I was taken. Xander made it sound like Jack and Luke hadn't been harmed or abducted, but if that's the case, why haven't they come for me yet? Where am I?

Xander stands with his back to me, his posture suggesting he's typing a message on his phone. I try to move my arms but I can barely wiggle them. Is it possible he tightened the knots while I was out? Or did the blood that seeped into the fibers make the rope swell? Either way, it's clear no amount of squirming will get me out of this. But maybe there's another way to get free.

Xander turns, his lips curving when his eyes land on me. "Look who's awake. You ready for round two, or have you reconsidered my offer?"

I'm not going to do what he wants, but I'm also not keen on another round of torture, so I try for distraction. "You haven't even explained what you want me to do."

His eyebrows arch. "Isn't it obvious? I need you to make more hybrids."

I snort. "I already told you—I don't know how I got to be this way."

"And I told you I don't think it's necessary to understand the mechanics. All my experiments have led me to one conclusion: *You* are the key."

I glare at him. "I have no interest in helping you with your experiments. Haven't enough innocent people died already?"

Instead of answering, Xander strolls over to one of the blanket-covered shapes along the wall and gives it a little kick. A metal grate rattles, followed by a low growling sound. "Did you know there are ways to keep a werewolf from shifting back to human form?" He smiles and shakes his head. "No, I don't imagine you would, being so new at this and all. It works in the other direction, too—which is why you can't shift now."

My stomach clenches. "Wait—are you saying you have a werewolf trapped under that blanket?"

His lips stretch in a leer and he pulls the cloth off with a flourish. Underneath is a plastic kennel, the kind people keep large dogs in. But there's something different about this one—a metallic gleam that takes me a minute to understand. A fine mesh covers every inch of the cage, and I can only imagine it's made out of silver to keep the wolf from being able to break through it. Through the grate, I detect movement. It's the glowing yellow eyes that I see first, but as the wolf moves closer, I catch a glimpse of her fur, her face. I recognize the soft gray color of her coat. It's Marisol, one of the pack members that split off to follow Mel.

I bear my teeth and a growl rumbles in my throat. "Let her go," I demand. How long has she been his prisoner? What happened to the other weres who split off with Mel? Rage bubbles in my veins and I struggle against the ropes despite the fact I know they won't give. I know she chose to leave my pack, but my wolf still sees her as family, and I want to get to her, to protect her.

Xander crosses his arms over his chest. "And why exactly would I do that? I need her. Just like I need you."

The ropes bite into my flesh as I pull against them. "I don't care what you do to me—I'm not going to help you."

He nods as if he expected this answer. "I figured

that already. I tried hurting you, and you showed surprising tenacity. Now, I could torture you some more—for days, in fact—but that would be a waste of precious time, and I'm not convinced it would break you anyway. So we're going to do this the easy way."

Before I can ask what he means, he whistles, and the vampires in the corner immediately turn off their game and jog to his side. The menacing glint in their eyes tells me they expect whatever Xander has in mind to be more entertaining than what they were already doing.

One of the girls throws a blanket off a smaller nearby box. There is no kennel underneath—only a large storage bin. She reaches her arm into it and pulls out some kind of gun. I'm the first to admit I don't know much about weapons, but this one doesn't look like any rifle or shotgun I'm familiar with. It's not until the girl hands the weapon and a small plastic box to Xander that I realize why: It's a tranquilizer gun.

"Now, weres metabolize things pretty quickly, so my friends and I will have to move fast," he explains as if teaching some kind of lesson. He opens the small box and removes a dart. As he loads it, his companions squirm with anticipation.

Even in her wolf form, Marisol seems to understand what comes next won't be good. She backs away from the front of the kennel, but all Xander does is smile.

A weight settles in my stomach. I try to tell myself that if Marisol had stayed with the pack, she wouldn't be here now. If she hadn't chosen to turn against us and side with Mel, we could have protected her. But no matter how I word the argument, I can't convince myself she deserves what's about to happen.

No matter her choices, I still see her as the girl who offered to show me around the enclave, who told me becoming a wolf was the best thing that ever happened to her. She may have chosen to join Mel, but that doesn't make her any less a part of my pack.

Xander fires the dart, and Marisol yelps. "Leave her alone!" I yell as the two guys walk over to the kennel. One of them is wearing a pair of leather gloves to avoid making contact with the silver overlay. He pulls the mesh away and opens the grate.

"Stop! Don't touch her!" I struggle against my bindings, but it's no use. The vampires continue as if they can't hear me.

Once the leather glove-wearing vampire tugs Marisol out of the kennel, he removes something from around her neck and she shifts into her human form. His friends step forward to help him pull her to a metal folding chair the blonde girl set up. The other girl stands nearby, holding a length of rope that I can tell even from here reeks of wolfsbane. Jack once referred to wolfsbane as inflicting pain he wouldn't wish on his worst enemy. If Marisol is bound with those ropes, they won't only keep her from breaking through them, they will likely sear her flesh and cause her excruciating pain. And I get the feeling that's not all Xander has in store for her.

"I'll do it!" I call. "I'll do whatever it is you want as long as you don't hurt her."

The girl holding the ropes drops her arms to her sides, her shoulders sagging as she gives a disappointed sigh. The guy in the leather gloves broods as he slips his hand into his back pocket and pulls out a bill, which he hands to Xander.

Xander smiles as he pockets the money. "Kyle here thought I was foolish and overestimated the strength of the bonds that connect you dogs." He jerks his chin at the kennel, and Kyle and the other guys drag Marisol's limp body back toward it. "Quickly now. We've only got about a minute before she wakes up again." He glances at the blonde. "Get the other one."

My heart pounds as the girl crosses to the other side of the room to another kennel-sized shape obscured by a blanket. "Who's in there?"

Xander tilts his head. "Consider him a test subject."

I combat the panic rising in my chest as the girl opens the kennel and pulls out a man I don't recognize. He appears to be about my age, and the dazed expression on his face is enough for me to know he's been drugged with something to keep him compliant. I inhale. Now that he's no longer hidden away, I can smell that he's human. "What do you want me to do?"

"I thought it was rather obvious. I want you to turn him into a hybrid." His lips curl.

"I don't know how."

"All you need to do is bite him." Xander says. "Do you know how vampires and werewolves turn people? Vampires inject a human with their venom. It doesn't happen every time we bite someone—it has to be a conscious decision. I think that's by design. If vampires injected everyone they ever bit with their venom, we'd have a lot more vampires on our hands—which in some ways would be cool, until the food supply ran low." He joins the blonde and helps guide the test subject closer to me. "Werewolves, on the other hand, spread the virus that made them with every bite. But since they don't go around chewing on humans, it's not that big of an issue. Now, if I'm right, all you need to do is bite our friend here. Your special venom laced with the werewolf virus should be the special ingredient we need to make him like you."

I stare at the guy they bring closer to me. I had thought he was about my age—nineteen or so—but now I think I was wrong. He looks younger, maybe seventeen. He should be making plans for his senior year of high school and figuring out which colleges to apply to. He shouldn't be here. Rage bubbles inside me. What right does Xander have to rip this boy out of his life? If he wants to go around killing vampires, that's one thing. But this boy deserves to live.

Xander's eyebrows draw together as he nears me. "You've got that look on your face," he says, narrowing his eyes. "That look like you're trying to figure a way out of this. Let me tell you how this is going to go down: I'm gonna bring this boy to you, and you're gonna bite him. If you don't, I'm gonna pull your friend Marisol out of her cage and we're going to torture her. And then you're gonna bite this kid. Either way, you're turning him into a hybrid."

My eyes flick toward Marisol's cage. Xander was right about the tranquilizer wearing off quickly: She's already awake, watching the events unfold beyond her kennel grate with wary eyes. I know Xander's not bluffing. I could refuse to bite this kid, but he'll just hurt Marisol. And if I refuse again, what's to keep him from killing her? And if he kills her and I still won't do what he asks, what's to keep him from finding more people to torture and kill—

more friends of mine?

I lock my eyes on Xander's. "If I do this, you'll let me go home?"

A self-satisfied smirk spreads itself across his face. "That was always the deal."

I gulp. "Okay, I'll do it."

Xander glances at his companion, who flashes a grin. The two of them bring the boy within arm's length of me. His eyes are glazed, and I wonder if he has any idea what's going on or what's about to happen to him. Xander and his companion lower the boy to his knees in front of me. He's tall and lanky, and this position puts him at just the right angle for me to access his neck. At this distance, his scent overwhelms me. His natural odor indicates he hasn't bathed in a few days, though I detect a hint of a musky body wash on his skin. But that's not what distracts me. I see the pulse of his vein beneath the flesh on his neck, and the scent of his blood fills my nostrils. The familiar burning sensation in my teeth lets me know my incisors are lengthening. This isn't like before, when I've fed from deer—it's more like the moment I knew I needed to drink from Jack.

My mind clouds. How long has it been since I've fed? Even if it had been earlier today, before the work my body had to do repairing itself after the car crash and the torture, I get the feeling my reaction would still be intense. It isn't just need fueling me now—it's desire.

My eyes prickle, and even in his subdued state, the boy registers enough surprise to let me know my irises are flashing red. I open my mouth and sink my teeth into his neck. Breaking the skin takes no effort at all, and I begin lapping the thick liquid in an instant. It's so good—better than anything I've ever tasted in my life—human or now. The warm sensation trickling down my throat satisfies me and at the same time makes me want more. I drink long, deep gulps; I hear muffled sounds, but none of them make any sense. Then the boy begins to jostle. He's fighting me, but how can he be? He's been drugged, and he doesn't seem to have enough self-awareness to put up much of a struggle. But then hands clamp around my throat, forcing my head backward. I snap and gnash my teeth as the boy's neck is pulled away from me.

"Easy there," Xander says, not quite hiding the smile curling his lips. "That was just supposed to be a simple bite. Don't want to drain him of too much before he goes through the change."

My incisors burn again as they shrink back to their normal size. With a nod from Xander, the person behind me releases me. My eyes land on the boy, whom the two guys have dragged to a safe distance and laid on the threadbare carpet. Blood stains the collar of his shirt, and his neck is smeared with red. Shame settles in my stomach. I did that. And what's worse, I couldn't have stopped myself if I'd wanted to.

Xander's vampire friends make their way back over to their makeshift gaming area. Xander smiles as he surveys me. "Now we wait."

"That wasn't the deal," I say quickly. "You said if I bit him you'd let me go."

He lets out a short laugh. "Not so fast. First we have to make sure my theory is right. So until he wakes up, you may as well make yourself comfortable."

CHAPTER TWENTY-SEVEN

I WAKE to the sound of raspy, gulping breaths. It takes me a minute to get my bearings, but when I remember where I am, my stomach twists violently and I have to swallow the bile rising in my throat.

I'm still in Xander's hideout, and the boy I bit—the one I would have sucked dry if not for intervention—is writhing on the threadbare carpet in front of me. I don't have a concept of how long it's been, but enough time has passed that I drifted off, still bound to this chair.

But for me and the boy—and likely Marisol in her covered kennel—the room is empty. I'm not sure where the video-gamers are, and I don't see Xander anywhere. Is it possible they all left? No, I can't imagine that's the case. This boy—what he is to become—is too important to Xander for him to leave us behind. The boy coughs, expelling droplets of spittle from his mouth. But that's not all it is. Even in this low light, I can see well enough to detect the pink tinge. He's choking up blood.

There's movement in the left corner of the room. Xander rushes in, his face alight with expectation, but as he nears, his expression darkens.

"No. No, no, no!" Xander kneels beside the boy, smoothing his sweaty hair off his forehead. The look is almost tender—almost. But instead of the sadness in the eyes of someone watching a person they care about in pain, there is only disappointment and anger.

The boy coughs some more, but each time the sound is weaker. His flailing grows less intense with each passing moment. When his chest rises and falls for the last time, Xander stands, his eyes fixing on me. "What did you do?"

It takes a minute for me to tear my gaze from the boy. What *have* I done? Did I just trade that boy's life for Marisol's? That poor young human boy. My eyes prickle with tears. What will his family think when he never comes home? "I did what you asked."

Xander stalks toward me. He raises his arm and brings the back of his hand down hard across my cheek. "Does that look like what I wanted?" he asks, pointing at the boy's lifeless body. "I wanted you to turn him into a hybrid, not kill him."

My cheek burns, but the pain is no less than I deserve. I blink, and tears spill onto my face. "I told you I didn't know how to do it. Don't blame me that it didn't work."

Xander begins pacing, one hand cupping the top of his head. "This should've worked," he says, more to himself than me. "It makes sense it wouldn't work on a vampire, but a human is a blank slate. This should have worked." He stops, turning and staring right at me. "Unless..."

I don't know what he's thinking. If he believes I did something wrong when I bit the boy, what might he do to me? More torture, I imagine. Even after this failure, I don't think he intends to kill me.

He pivots and strides toward the large storage container his friend went to earlier. He's going for the tranquilizer gun.

Marisol. Is he going to hurt her because I failed? "It's not her fault. She has nothing to do with this," I say as he crosses to Marisol's kennel.

He ignores me. He shoulders the gun and fires it. A small yelp is all it takes for me to know he's hit his mark.

"Torturing her will get you nothing," I continue. "She's not the one you want—I am. If you think I did something wrong, hurt me. Leave her alone!"

He completely ignores me as he returns the gun to its bin and removes a pair of leather gloves. After slipping them on, he opens the kennel and drags out Marisol's limp body. "I've been going about this all wrong," he murmurs. "A human may be pure, but it doesn't have the strength to become what you are."

I begin to understand what he's thinking. "But I was human, and I survived," I say. I don't know what I intend to prove with my observation. I don't want any more innocent humans to be subjected to my bite, but I don't like the idea of the alternative, either.

"I don't know what it is about you. Maybe we'll never know." He drags Marisol's body closer to me. "Maybe it was when you got bitten or how you were killed, or maybe it's something special about you in particular. Hell, maybe it was the phase of the moon. But if a vampire can't be turned, and a human can't be, that leaves one alternative." He pulls Marisol and holds her so she's nearly on my lap. "Bite her."

I shake my head. "I don't want any more blood on my hands."

Xander's eyes flash red. "Bite her, or watch me rip out her heart."

I gulp, weighing my options. Only one of those two outcomes isn't a surefire death sentence.

He holds up his hand like a claw and brings it

down on her back. Even in her unconscious state, Marisol twitches and lets out a moan as his fingers dig into her skin. "I'm not a patient man."

I'm out of time. "Fine! I'll do it—just don't kill her."

Xander smirks, removing his nails from her flesh. "Okay, so get on with it."

I stare down at Marisol's neck, but there's no burning in my teeth. I've never tried to make my incisors grow on command before. Any time it's happened, it's been due to hunger or need, neither of which I'm feeling now. If I focus, I can detect a faint smell of her blood pulsing under her flesh, but it doesn't affect me the same way the promise of human blood did.

"Come on already," Xander snarls.

"I'm sorry, I'm kind of new at this."

A muscle in his jaw jumps. "What's the problem?"

I pull back my lips, bearing my teeth. He releases an irritated sigh before shifting Marisol's weight and dragging one nail across her neck. Rivulets of blood spring up in its wake. The simple sight of the blood is enough to make my teeth lengthen. Although there's no overwhelming desire to bite her, I bring my mouth to her neck anyway. I feel the venom seep from my gums and I hold on, making sure to allow it to pass into her vein. When

I'm sure I've done my part, I pull away.

Xander looks down at me approvingly. "This will do nicely," he says, smiling down at me.

I run my tongue over my teeth as they shrink down to normal size. "I suppose it's too much to hope that you'd let me go now."

He drags Marisol across the floor and deposits her a few feet away from the boy's body. "Same deal as before," he says. "If she wakes up a hybrid, you're free to go."

"And if she doesn't?"

He narrows his eyes. "For your sake, let's hope it doesn't come to that."

I'M NOT SURE how many hours have passed when the blonde girl approaches me. Her steps are precise, apprehensive, and she holds a red plastic cup out toward me.

"Do you need water?"

At first, I'm struck by the way she says it—almost like she's unsure. It takes me a moment to realize why. Vampires probably don't need anything but blood to survive. Since I'm a hybrid, the same doesn't hold true for me. "That would be nice," I say. Besides the boy's blood, I don't know the last time I ingested anything. My mouth is dry, and when she tips the water past my lips, it spills down my throat, offering a reprieve. "Thank you," I say when she removes the cup.

Her lip twitches. "I don't get it," she murmurs.

"Don't get what?"

Her eyes widen a fraction of an inch, like she's surprised she spoke out loud. She shakes her head. "I don't see why he wants to make more like you."

I do my best to shrug. "Your guess is as good as mine."

Before she can say more, Xander reenters the room from what I imagine is a doorway in the left corner. The girl backs away from me as Xander crosses to Marisol's side. Thankfully, they removed the boy's body some time ago. My only hope now is that Marisol won't join him in whatever shallow grave he's in.

Xander crouches beside Marisol and checks her pulse. The smile that spreads across his lips is enough to loosen the knot in my chest. "She's not dead yet," Xander says.

I shift in my chair. "Does that mean I can leave?"

He arches an eyebrow. "I'm optimistic, not foolish."

I figured it was a long shot, but given my current circumstances, it couldn't hurt to ask. "The transition could take days, couldn't it?"

"Let's hope it doesn't."

The blonde returns hours later with more water and a handful of almonds. After allowing me to drink, she pops a nut into my mouth and offers a faint smile. "It's been so long since I've had to eat food I couldn't figure out what to bring you."

I chew and swallow. "This is fine. Thank you."

She pokes another almond through my lips. "I figure Xander doesn't want you to die before he's had a successful subject."

There's no one else in the room. Xander has been checking on Marisol regularly, but he and the rest of the video-gamers have been gone for a while. "You don't seem to care if he makes more hybrids. Why are you helping him?"

She raises her eyebrows. "I'm not willing to risk the alternative. Sure, right now he's convinced there's no way to turn a vampire into a hybrid, but who's to say he won't change his mind? I'm not interested in being one of his subjects."

My mind spins with this new information. Whatever Xander's end game is, this girl isn't a part of it. If her goal is self-preservation, I might be able to exploit it. "Do you know Luke? Are you a member of his brood?"

Surprise flickers across her face, but she hides it quickly. "Yes."

I swallow, choosing my words carefully. "He

came to my territory and offered to help protect me. In return, he's been given lodging in the enclave. If you release me—help me escape—I can plead your case to get the same kind of deal for you."

Her mouth twitches as she processes the offer, but before she can answer, Marisol stirs. My heartbeat ratchets up. She's writhing the same way the boy did before he died. The boy. I don't even know his name.

The blonde stands and puts distance between the two of us. "Xander!"

He's in the room in an instant. He rushes to Marisol, making sure to keep his distance in case she strikes out. Marisol turns from side to side as if stuck in a nightmare. After several moments, Xander reaches out a hand and shakes her shoulder.

She's upright in a flash, her hand clamped around his wrist. When her eyes open, they flash gold, and my stomach clenches. Did it not work? At the very least, she's not dead—so that's a step in the right direction.

But before my mind can spin with too many possibilities, her irises shift to a glowing red.

"Simone!" he calls, and the blonde moves a few steps closer. "I think our friend might need something to drink."

Simone nods before darting from the room.

Xander turns his attention to Marisol and attempts to extricate his arm from her grip. “Hey, now. You need to calm down. I have no intention of hurting you.”

She glares at him for a moment longer before releasing him. “What have you done to me?”

Xander smiles. “I’ve made you better.”

Simone returns, another red cup in hand, but this one doesn’t contain water. My teeth burn, but I do my best to ignore the smell of blood. When Simone hands Marisol the cup, Marisol stares at its contents. “What am I supposed to do with this?”

Xander positions himself directly in front of her, forcing her to look into his eyes. “I suggest you drink it if you want to live.”

For moment, Marisol looks like she’d like nothing better than to throw the cup across the room, but then her expression goes blank. It seems her transition to hybrid hasn’t given her protection against Xander’s compulsion. Her irises turn red again and she brings the cup to her lips.

“Good. You drink that, then sit there like a good girl.” As she greedily gulps down the blood, Xander jumps to his feet and rubs his hands together as he approaches me. “It worked.”

“I see that,” I say. I nod toward the ropes around my forearms. “You ready to untie me?”

He shakes his head. “Not even close.”

"That was the deal," I growl through clenched teeth.

He shrugs. "Unfortunately for you, I don't know yet if this hybrid you made can make more. But I know for a fact you can. You've got work to do before I can let you go."

Before I can answer, Xander turns and lets out a whistle. Moments later, the rest of his companions enter the room. "We've had a success," he says, motioning toward Marisol. "Now I need you to bring me more wolves."

The guys rub their hands together eagerly while one girl smiles. Only the blonde, Simone, looks at all uneasy. Still, she joins the others as they make their way toward the back corner of the room. The fact that they need to leave this space—and possibly the building—is both comforting and distressing. On the one hand, it's possible they don't have more weres—more former members of my pack—imprisoned on the grounds. On the other, I have no way of knowing how long it will take them to find more weres for me to turn.

"That's your master plan, then?" I call, louder than is strictly necessary, before the other vampires are out of earshot. "You're going to make me turn more weres into hybrids? When does it end? Do you want to turn them all into what I am?"

Simone and two of the guys pause and glance

back at us, their eyebrows raised with interest. Do any of them know what Xander's end game really is? Or are they on his side out of self-preservation only?

"It's no concern of yours," Xander says. He waves his hand dismissively at those who have stopped to listen, but they don't immediately move on.

"I guess you're right," I say, taking advantage of my opportunity. The more time Xander spends talking with me—the more time his minions are listening—the fewer weres I'll be forced to bite. "It seems you've got everything figured out. Force me to make hybrids—submissive ones you can control. But what if that doesn't work? Or what if you mess up and make me turn a wolf who's not so easy to compel? Or what if one comes across her alpha and his commands override yours?"

Xander shakes his head. "You're just trying to distract me, and you're trying to confuse them. You dogs can break away from an alpha, and if I have to compel all of them to do so before you bite them, so be it." He turns to his companions. "Go—get more dogs and bring them here. Now."

Before any of them can move, a crash reverberates through the room, emanating from the door in the back corner. Xander curses. He points toward the source of the noise. "Go check it out.

Simone, grab the new hybrid. I'll take care of this one."

He strides toward me and I gulp, not sure exactly what he intends to do, but the wooden door in the corner splinters and cracks and six wolves charge into the room. My heart swells when I see the one leading the group. The markings on his coat are unmistakable. Jack. He came for me. I knew he would.

The vampires hiss as the invading weres lunge at them. Xander obscures my view of the fight as he crouches in front of me, his fingers skimming the ropes binding me to the chair. He glances over his shoulder and his muscles tense. I'm sure I know what's going through his mind. Obviously he'd like to get me out of here, away from my rescuers, but if I can't break through these ropes, there's no way he'll be able to. An internal struggle plays itself out across his features for a few fractions of a second before he darts into the fray.

Kyle and the other vampire guy square off against Lillie, Sawyer, and Angela. Dakota and Duncan snap their jaws menacingly at the female vampire with short hair. Jack runs for me, but Xander blocks him.

Simone struggles to pull Marisol to her feet. Xander's compulsion must be strong, because Marisol can't manage to make her legs support her weight. With a frustrated growl, Simone bends down and loops her arms around Marisol's thighs, shouldering her like a bag of potatoes.

She's going to take Marisol away to who knows where. I can't let her do that—there's no telling what these vampires might make her do. "Jack! Get Marisol!"

He's distracted by my words for only a split second, but it's long enough for Xander to land a solid blow across Jack's muzzle. He's knocked off balance and Xander exploits the moment of weakness by kicking Jack in the ribs. I shout, rage bubbling inside me. I want to tear through these ropes and rip off Xander's head for daring to hurt my half.

Jack is doing his best to get back to his paws, but it's clear Xander's blow knocked the wind out of him. Xander's fingers curl into claws and I know what he intends to do as he closes the distance between himself and Jack. I need to alert someone to what's about to happen, but my mind spins and I can't find the words. As Xander raises his hand in preparation to strike, a scream rips itself from my throat. I don't want to watch what will happen next, but I can't look away.

As Xander brings his claws down toward Jack's chest, a blur appears from out of nowhere and knocks him over. Xander crashes to the floor, his eyes wide with surprise as they fix on his attacker.

Luke.

"Don't mess with my little brother," he snarls. In a flash, he lunges toward Xander. A shriek of pain is cut short and a moment later, Luke stands, blood soaking his tee-shirt, Xander's disembodied head suspended from his hand by its hair.

The other vampires freeze as the scent of blood reaches them. Then, without hesitation, Kyle leads the others in retreat. Sawyer and Angela give chase, but I shout before Lillie, Duncan, and Dakota can follow. "A girl named Simone has Marisol. You need to get her—they made me—" I squeeze my eyes closed. "She's a hybrid."

There's only a brief hesitation in Dakota's step before she nods and leads Duncan back out the way they came. Lillie hovers awkwardly until Jack shifts to human and beckons for her to follow him. She shifts, too, and offers a watery smile as she makes her way toward me.

Jack is at my side in a moment and he begins pulling at the ropes, growling when they don't break.

"They're Kevlar," I explain. I lift my chin toward the bin beyond Marisol's kennel. "There might be something in there to cut through it."

Wordlessly, Luke starts for the box.

Lillie crouches beside Jack, her fingers

brushing the blood-soaked fabric of my shirt and the red-stained ropes holding me in place. "What did they do to you?"

The corners of my mouth twitch. "Nothing that hasn't been done before. Believe it or not, being stabbed isn't nearly so bad after you've already been through it." I try to smile, but my lips can't quite make the shape. I wiggle my fingers, and Lillie takes the hint and curls her hand around them. "I didn't expect to see you on the rescue team."

"She wouldn't take no for an answer," Jack murmurs. He strokes a finger down my cheek, his eyes dark with emotion. "Sorry it took us so long."

My eyes prickle and I blink in an attempt to keep the tears from falling. I want to tell him it's okay, but the words won't come. I lean forward as far as I can and Jack makes up the rest of the distance, pressing his lips to mine.

We pull apart only when Luke clears his throat beside us. "These should work," he says, holding out a heavy-looking pair of shears. "I recommend you save the reunion for when you're back in wolf world."

Jack cuts through the cords around my right arm first, and as soon as it's free, I reach for Luke's arm. "Thank you."

He presses his lips into a tight line and nods.

"Those vampires made you make another

hybrid?" Lillie asks as Jack continues freeing me.

I nod. "I'm still not entirely sure why, but yes."

Jack cuts through the last of the cords and scoops me into his arms. I think I could probably walk, but I'm glad he's not making me find out. "Let's worry about that later. First, let's get you home."

CHAPTER TWENTY-EIGHT

I WAS MISSING just over two days, but when we make it back to the enclave, it feels like I've been away much longer. Jack wants me to get straight to bed to rest and recover from my ordeal, but I refuse. I can't just lie around—not when there are still so many unanswered questions. Jack only relents when Luke points out they need any information I can give them about what Xander and his cronies were up to.

I'm stationed on the couch in Jack's living room with a quilt over my legs. Every time I try to take it off, Lillie gives me the evil eye and tucks it back in, so I eventually give up.

As the adrenaline from the rescue ebbs, hunger grows in the pit of my stomach. While Jack heads into the kitchen to make me some food, Luke swipes a mug from a cupboard and slips out of the house for about ten minutes. He returns just as Jack settles a tray loaded with eggs, bacon, toast, and fruit across my lap. Under his brother's watchful eye, Luke places the mug in the upper right corner of the tray.

"Don't worry—I didn't kill anything," he mutters, his eyes sliding to Jack.

"Thank you," I murmur. While the breakfast-for-dinner Jack prepared looks and smells wonderful, I'm getting to know myself well enough to be sure it won't be sufficient to satisfy all my body's needs after what I went through. I'm glad for Luke's presence—for the fact that he anticipated my need and didn't make me ask.

Lillie pulls her feet up onto her chair and slips them under her thighs. Although she tries to keep her face neutral, her nose wrinkles when I take a sip from the mug. The blood has an effect on me immediately, replenishing a measure of my strength as soon as I swallow it. But I'm the one who fights to keep my face impassive at the taste. It's from a deer—something I should be used to by now. But after tasting human blood, it's all I can do not to frown at the flavor.

Jack waits until Luke takes a seat before speaking. "Xander was the one in charge of everything?"

I swallow a bite of eggs. "Yes. From what I could tell, the others mostly didn't want to end up as test subjects."

"Any idea why he wanted to make more hybrids at all?" Luke asks. "I'll be the first to admit, the two of us were never close, but he never struck me as the kind of guy who longed to have an army at his command."

I close my eyes for a moment as images of Xander brandishing a knife flash through my head. "He said something about being sick of being policed by weres. Maybe he thought if he had some hybrids on his side, they could keep the werewolves from bothering him."

Jack sighs. "We'll never know exactly what he had in mind."

Luke pulls back his shoulders, his posture defensive. "Would you rather I'd let him kill you?"

"I didn't say that." Jack crosses his arms over his chest. "Thank you, by the way."

Luke cups his hand around his ear. "I'm sorry, what was that?"

Lillie and I exchange glances and she hides a smile behind her hand. "So, what's our next move?" I ask. As entertaining as it is watching the brothers bicker, we have more important matters to attend to. "We have to find Marisol, right?" My throat tightens and I struggle to swallow around the lump that's formed there.

"That's the sire bond you're feeling," Luke murmurs. "It's stronger when you accept responsibility for a vampire you've created. As I'm learning."

My stomach flutters at his words. Does he feel the same protectiveness for me that's brimming inside me for Marisol? I have an overwhelming desire to make sure she's safe. Is that what caused Luke to venture to the outskirts of the territory and offer assistance to the wolves, despite the fact he expected to be treated like a prisoner?

Jack studies Luke out of the corner of his eye before speaking. "As much as I'd like to believe she's like you and doesn't pose a threat, the fact is we don't know that for sure. And if the witches catch wind that another hybrid exists—and that you had a hand in making her..."

I nod. "Yeah, it won't be good."

I'm finishing my meal when there's a knock at Jack's door. Dakota and Duncan enter, and I can tell before they speak that the news isn't good.

"We lost her," Dakota says, not meeting Jack's eye.

"Head to the meeting house," he says, his tone even. "Lillie, go with them. I want you to coordinate a set of search parties to be on rotation until Marisol is found."

The three weres nod and exit, leaving me alone with Jack and Luke. "I should probably go, too," Jack says, lifting his chin toward the door.

"I'll come," I say, pulling the blanket off my legs now that Lillie isn't here to insist I keep it on.

He shakes his head. "I promise you can be as involved in the search as you want tomorrow. Tonight, you should rest." He strides to my side and holds his hand out to me. "I'll take you home on my way."

I raise my hand but hesitate before slipping it into his. Although I'm probably safer here in the enclave than I am anywhere else, the idea of going to my empty house is unsettling. Since Cassandra's arrival, Lillie has been spending most nights at Maggie's house to help with overnight care. After what I just went through, I don't want to be alone. "Would it be okay if I stayed here tonight?"

Jack drops his hand and kneels so he's at eye level with me. "Always." He leans in to kiss me before raising himself back to his full height. "I won't be gone long." He strides toward the door, pausing briefly to address Luke. "Can you keep her company until I get back?"

"Sure," Luke says quietly. His eyes linger on Jack until he disappears behind the front door. He's silent for a few moments before turning to me. "Congratulations, by the way."

I raise my eyebrows. “For what?”

“You know.” He waves his hand toward the door. “I don’t know what the right thing is to say to someone who’s found her half.”

Heat creeps into my cheeks. I’ve moved beyond feeling embarrassed by the idea, and I’ve accepted just how important Jack is to me, but for some reason, having Luke talk about it makes me uncomfortable. “Um, thanks.”

“I’m happy for you. And Jack deserves something like this—something good.” His gaze drops. “He’s had more than his fair share of bad.”

I get the feeling he wants to say more, but he doesn’t go on. Part of me wants to ask, but another part wonders if I need to know. Jack doesn’t like to dwell on the past, and it’s not my place to make him. I clear my throat and stand. “I think I’ll get to bed.”

Before I’ve taken more than a couple of steps, Luke is at my side. He slips an arm around my waist and helps me toward the hall. “Don’t worry—I’m not going to try anything,” he assures me as he pushes open the bedroom door. “Earlier today, when I was dealing with Xander, Jack had this look in his eyes that I haven’t seen in... well, in about a century.”

We reach the bed and he helps lower me onto the mattress. “Really? What was the look?”

Luke pulls the sheet and blanket across my

body as I lean against the pillow. "Like he was seeing his brother." He smooths the comforter before turning toward the door. "Goodnight, Ava."

"Goodnight," I say as he exits the room.

I sigh, relaxing my muscles. It'll be good to sleep in a bed, and even better to be snuggled next to Jack. There are dangers to take care of, but they'll still be there tomorrow. We need to find Marisol, and we need to make sure there aren't any more vampires like Xander out there who want to create more hybrids. But I'm confident we can figure it out.

I'm still awake when Jack slides into bed beside me. He drapes his arm across my waist and buries his face in my hair. I'm convinced he thinks I'm asleep for a solid minute before he speaks.

"You know we'll find her, right?"

My lips twitch and my eyes prickle. "She didn't ask to be what I am."

"*You* didn't ask to be what you are." He pulls me closer to him. "Xander's gone. Marisol's probably just scared and confused. But once that passes, she'll come find you. We'll figure out a way to explain to the witches' council what happened, and they'll realize you're not at fault."

I run my fingers along his bicep. "You sound so certain."

"Certain? No. Optimistic." His hand skims up

my body until it cups my face. "The only thing I'm certain about is us."

I shift until I'm on my side. The waning moonlight slanting through his bedroom window highlights the planes and valleys of his face. "I feel the same way."

I lean forward tentatively, and when he brushes his lips against mine, the last of the tension and fear I was holding on to fades away. I'm still worried about Marisol and concerned that there might be others out there ready to take up Xander's cause, but I also know Jack will do everything in his power to keep me safe. Our troubles didn't end today, but when we wake up tomorrow to face them, we'll do it together.

ABOUT THE AUTHOR

Madeline Freeman lives in the metro-Detroit area with her husband, her daughter and son, and her cats. She loves anything to do with astronomy, outer space, plate tectonics, and dinosaurs, and secretly hopes her kids will become astronomers or paleontologists.

Connect with Madeline online:
http://www.madelinefreeman.net
http://twitter.com/writer_maddie
http://facebook.com/madelinefreemanbooks

Sign up for Madeline's reader's group for updates and exclusive content!

http://smarturl.it/MFMailingList-2

ALSO BY MADELINE FREEMAN

Clearwater Witches Series

Crystal Magic

Wild Magic

Circle Magic

Moon Magic

Cursed Magic

Dark Magic

The Naturals Trilogy

Awaking

Seeking

Becoming

Shifted Series

Shifted

Tangled

Twisted

Made in the USA
Las Vegas, NV
30 August 2021